Michel Déon, who was born in P[illegible]ay in 2016 at the age of 97, was [illegible]orks of fiction and non-fiction[illegible]mie Française.

Julian Evans is a writer and translator from French and German. He has previously translated Michel Déon's *The Foundling Boy*, *The Foundling's War* and *The Great and the Good*.

Praise for the Foundling novels:

'Remarkable ... deserves a place alongside Flaubert's *Sentimental Education* and *Le Grand Meaulnes*'
New Statesman

'A big-hearted coming-of-age shaggy-dog story ... [Déon's] novel leaves you feeling better about life' *The Spectator*

'It is shamefully parochial of us that this eminent writer has been so ignored by the anglophone world' *Sunday Times*

'Quiet, wryly funny prose ... a delight'
Independent on Sunday

'Déon is an outrageous storyteller, a most engaging tease and the result is a splendid mixture of acerbic asides and bright invention which reads admirably in Julian Evans's excellent translation.' *Times Literary Supplement*

Your Father's Room

Michel Déon

translated from the French by Julian Evans

Your Father's Room

Michel Déon

translated from the French by Julian Evans

Gallic Books
London

This book is supported by the Institut français (Royaume-Uni) as part of the Burgess Programme (www.frenchbooknews.com).

INSTITUT
FRANÇAIS
ROYAUME-UNI

A Gallic Book

First published in France as *La chambre de ton père* by Éditions Gallimard, 2004

First published in Great Britain in 2017 by
Gallic Books, 59 Ebury Street,
London, SW1W 0NZ

A CIP record for this book is available from the British Library
ISBN 978-1-910477-34-2

Typeset in Fournier MT by Gallic Books
Printed in the UK by CPI (CR0 4TD)
2 4 6 8 10 9 7 5 3 1

After all these general remarks,
I shall now be born.

Stendhal, *The Life of Henry Brulard*

His parents would tell him, 'You can't possibly remember. You weren't even a year old when we moved from the apartment in Rue de la Roquette.' But he was adamant, and even now, at his very great age, the perfection of the image remains. He can still see himself sitting in a pram at the foot of a winding staircase lit by a window on the landing. The carpet is bright red. Under the stair, a frosted glass door opens and a short woman dressed in black, neither young nor old, looks at him. He remembers the name of the concierge who came over to talk to him only because he was told what it was when he recalled the memory later. Her name was Madame Lebas. She looked after him when his parents went out for the evening, which they did often.

Later, although he wondered about the scene so precisely etched in his memory, he refused to see a psychiatrist specialising in infantile recall. He merely accepted it as a flash of clarity that for some unknown reason had embedded itself in his baby memory, imprinting an indelible colour image there, an image that, incidentally, was completely unimportant and one he would have loved to replace with another – of his mother and father bending over his cradle, for example, or kissing each other. As the years went by, following several dreams in which he seemed to split in two and be able to watch himself, he conceived a theory that might have been plausible: that the soul – or in any case the immaterial, impenetrable thing that stands in for the soul – likes to divest itself of the body it inhabits occasionally and to contemplate its empty physical form, either out of impatience at being held captive by a child whose speech, sight and physical coordination are still in a larval state, or because that same physical form, despite being grown-up and perfectly comfortable with itself, is immersed for several hours in the torpor of sleep, which prevents it from reacting, other than by moans and groans, to the incoherent, absurd language of dreams. It should be added that the soul never goes far away, two or three metres at most, for fear that in its absence the sensory life of its protégé might suddenly be extinguished, a phenomenon that does sometimes occur in the course of such separations, to the bafflement of medical science. So wasn't it possible that the soul might exist from birth onwards in a perfectly functioning state, in possession of all its faculties, knowledge and memory, and sometimes go off on a short adventure to breathe the air of freedom and gain the necessary distance to perfect its awareness of things? That little adventure out of the way, it can then resume, in a baby's case, the process of educating the body it has been entrusted with, or the simple path of an existence that is already fully developed but perhaps just a touch monotonous.

He has never been able to call to mind the hall, the staircase with the red carpet, and Madame Lebas the concierge without a completely different scene following immediately – different because this time he is nearly two years old. They are living in a middle-class house in Châtenay (that detail filled in some time later), and, in a room that has its curtains drawn, a white sheet has been hung over a big Norman wardrobe. A copper-and-gold magic lantern stands on a console table; Papa is selecting coloured glass slides that he slips into the machine's innards. And who appears on the white sheet? Pulcinella himself, with his hunchback, his beak-like nose and his extravagant hat sewn with bells. The scene is as sharp as it was nearly eighty years ago. There must have been other performances, other glass slides, showing the wicked fairy Carabosse, the wizard Merlin, and Sleeping Beauty, but Pulcinella is the only one whose grotesque figure, imprinted on his memory as he leant back into a large bosom, has remained. A warm hand had clasped his tightly. Later, photographs provided the round face, pulled-back hair and solid frame of his nanny: Madeleine Schmidt.

From Châtenay he also has, from what must be around the same time, the image of his father naked to the waist, face covered with lather, shaving himself with a cutthroat razor and singing off-key a tune of Paul Delmet's, 'Sending Flowers'. The little boy takes hold of the razor, lying on the rim of the basin, and slashes his left hand deeply at the base of his thumb. Blood spurts from the cut. Papa lifts the boy, who neither shouts nor cries, onto his shoulders, dashes out into the street in his pyjama bottoms and races in the direction of the chemist's, where he bursts through the door with blood running through his hair and down his face. Only now does the little boy, thinking his father has been hurt, start shouting and burst into tears.

At this point the memory box closes shut, but to prove that it is all true he still has, just at the base of his thumb, the scar that for the rest of his life he cannot see without also seeing his father's bloodied head as he ran at breakneck speed down the empty street with him on his shoulders.

There are no more memories of Châtenay, apart from

those that can be re-assembled from sepia photos: of him standing on a round table in the garden, and of Madeleine holding his hand. He wonders whether in those early years he really loved anyone but her. Or snapshots, still relatively sharp despite their age, of his parents, his father in white trousers with shirtsleeves rolled up and a sleeveless cardigan, racquet in hand on the tennis court with her, Blanche, and two extremely pretty friends wearing the black headbands that were fashionable at the time, a detail memorialised in a pastel drawing of Blanche that still hangs on the wall in his study. During one of his moves the drawing, carelessly packed, had been damaged, and afterwards the picture framer had only been able to save her head, but her son has not forgotten her posing with bare shoulders wrapped in a gauze scarf which scarcely hid her breasts.

Although he was four years old by the time they moved to Rue Henri-Heine in Paris, he hasn't a single memory of Madeleine there. She must have taken him to Ranelagh, carrying him up the stairs of the footbridge over the 'Little Belt' circular railway, watched him making his first mud pies, and picked him up when he fell off his scooter. But no. Nothing. Everything has been erased, until with a click the shutter opens again: leaning on the balcony with his mother and looking down, he sees Madeleine getting into a green Renault taxi with its hood down. She is going back to Alsace. Blanche says, 'Look at her. You won't see her again.' As the driver signals with his left hand to indicate that he is turning into Avenue Mozart, Madeleine turns round on the back seat and waves a handkerchief. He is sure she is crying.

His mother was wrong. Almost as soon as the war was over, in 1945, he had travelled to Alsace, going from parish to parish to find Madeleine, now married, with five children, of whom the eldest had recently died, clearing the road of landmines. She had recognised him instantly. They cried together. She was a solid woman in a grey smock with a gentle face that radiated such calm goodness, such clemency and generosity that later he put her into several of his books, under her real name or different names, but recognisable to him alone.

When had he realised he was called Teddy? For a long time it was just a sound that could mean either him or the dog who belonged to their neighbours across the landing. Sometimes he would answer with a bark, which at first made his parents laugh, then annoyed them so much that they smacked him, putting an end to his first attempt at humour. For some reason they did not appreciate humour where their son was concerned, and considered it to be a disappointing sign of idiocy. When the day came for him to go to school, he of course had to be told that outside of family and friends his name was Édouard, which was what his schoolmistress would call him. He discovered himself in a new incarnation, and that, by alternating his names, he changed his world. The mistress at the Petit Cours La Fontaine found that he had a talent for drawing straight lines, either vertical or leaning, with which he filled several exercise books. Indulgently she suggested he copy the alphabet that she had printed on the blackboard, which he obediently did with such ease that she wondered how much he had been making fun of her. One day the class was asked to learn a poem, and he missed out the first two lines:

Little schoolboy a-going to school,
Think how you are becoming time's fool…

14

The mistress summoned the recalcitrant pupil's mother.

'This child has memory lapses. I recommend he sees a doctor.'

Standing between the two women in the small courtyard, Teddy-Édouard, looking up, watches a gutter along which a male pigeon is pursuing a female. He claps his hands and gives a war cry. The pigeons flap away. Interrupting his mother, who is upset and cross, he says 'a-going' is a mistake and if he's a fool, time's an even bigger one. Her brief humiliation avenged, Blanche takes him to a sweet shop and buys him a bar of Nestlé chocolate. If you take the bar carefully out of its wrapper and fold up the silver paper neatly 'for the little Chinese children',[1] when you've collected fifty wrappers you can send off for a coloured illustration of one of Monsieur de La Fontaine's fables. The sweet-shop lady has beautiful black eyes, a streak of white in her light-brown hair, and – a detail that does not escape Teddy's attention and even obsesses him mildly – a swollen index finger with a black nail that is peeling off. 'It happened drawing the curtains,' she says. Fifty times a day she has to reassure her customers, who are worried that she has some strange ailment. Maman retells the story of the poem at least as many times. Édouard is relegated to the back of the class, where he learns to read by himself so well that he brings his own book to school: *Memoirs of a Donkey*.[2] Outraged, Mademoiselle confiscates the handsome volume (a Bibliothèque Rose edition), but when she finds out what it's called she starts to laugh and holds it up for the rest of the class.

'Édouard has already written his memoirs!'

The class hoots with laughter and he cries a little, but not much, because there's a girl waiting for him at the gate: Yolande, who is studying for her baccalauréat in another class. He looks up to her admiringly, partly because of her height, but also because she holds his hand to walk him home to Rue Henri-Heine. He hears people say she is very pretty, and, studying her, he begins to develop his first idea of female beauty, even though many years later he is unable to remember anything about the way she looks. On the other hand, he can still conjure up quite clearly Yolande's mother, Madame N., the owner of their apartment in Rue Henri-Heine and of several buildings in Avenue Mozart. In a huge sitting room with scented oil lamps burning all around, a languid-looking woman is half lying on a sofa overflowing with damask cushions, a Pekinese on her knees, toying with an amber necklace and smoking mauve cigarettes with golden tips. She kisses him and lets him plunge his hand into a crystal bowl filled with chocolates. An aura of mystery surrounds her.

One day, when Maman is quarrelling with Papa, Maman says, 'Don't forget the reason we were able to get this apartment is because Madame N. was my brother's mistress.'

Yet the brother was a well-known man in Paris and in other countries, and often busy travelling, and you really couldn't see how someone like Madame N. would have been his teacher.

Why would Édouard remember so precisely the face of the sweet-shop lady at the corner of Rue du Ranelagh and Avenue Mozart, and not Mademoiselle's at the Petit Cours La Fontaine? He has even forgotten her name. In the subterranean activity that can wipe clean whole tracts of the past (and occasionally even of the day before), an obscure score-settling takes place: there are humiliations to be avenged, not to mention Papa's bad mood on discovering that his offspring has been answering his teacher back and correcting her.

'He's going to be a pedant! A bore!' he says.

Words that stick. The following year would be very different. The ground-floor classroom at an address in Rue Davioud is dark and there is no playground. Panels that cover the bottom half of the windows shield the pupils from the prying eyes of passers-by who can read in gilded letters the words 'Mademoiselle de Cordemoy – Private Tuition'. There are no more than a dozen pupils in what must once have been a sitting room from which the furniture has been removed and piled up in the lobby and down a corridor feebly illuminated by a fanlight. Placed in storage or sold, the missing pictures have left hooks and pale rectangles behind them on walls covered with beige crêpe paper that is slowly turning the colour of pee.

Mademoiselle de Cordemoy is a wizened old nag who wears a long black dress with a lace collar. Her dress is gathered at the waist with a rope belt, from which hangs a reticule in which she rummages nervously to find her handkerchief and dab her nostrils at each of her frequent sneezing fits. From the far end of the corridor in her apartment there comes, from time to time, amplified by the tunnel-like space blocked with chairs and old chests of drawers, the sound of moaning, of an inhuman howling. Putting down her ruler, which like a metronome beats out her lessons and dictations, or points to the map of France pinned to the wall to indicate each of the *départements* and its prefecture, Mademoiselle orders the children to be good and hurries out. They hear her stomping down the corridor like a policeman, calling out 'I'm coming!' They know Mademoiselle has a very sick brother. Their parents say it is her lifelong burden. She had been on the point of marrying a brilliant naval officer when an unknown bacterium paralysed her brother. Mademoiselle has sacrificed her life to save him from going to the paupers' hospital. He, of course, shows no gratitude for her sacrifice and bellows all day and night.

One evening at dinner time Papa suggests that this invisible brother might be the Minotaur. Teddy tells his classmates what Papa has said and inevitably there is one stupid boy who immediately puts his hand up in the middle of a lesson and asks, 'Is it true that your brother's called Minotaur?'

'No, little one, he's called Maurice. He's in a great deal of pain and he can't bear the light. Who told you about the Minotaur?'

'Teddy.'

Papa was sent a long-winded, half-serious letter in which Mademoiselle expressed herself delighted that, thanks to his parents, Teddy knew some mythology. Teddy was not allowed any pudding that night. Which is how children learn not to repeat the things that grown-ups say. But that was only the beginning.

Many years later, walking past his old classroom (long gone, the Cordemoys having vanished without trace), Édouard tries to remember the dozen pupils at the school, but can only bring two faces to mind. Girls, perhaps inevitably. The first was unforgettable: Évangeline de Something or other, fourteen or fifteen years old, twice as old as the next oldest pupil. In fact she was twice as much in everything, being so fat that she took up the whole of a double desk and her frame sagged under the weight of a pair of breasts that were phenomenal for her age. When she came to school, as she sometimes did, without her wild, frizzy hair tied under a cotton turban, Évangeline obscured half the class. Her complexion was a little darker than coffee-coloured, and when she opened her mouth she revealed wonderful teeth. When she sat down Mademoiselle would admonish her.

'Put your knees together, young lady!'

But with thighs the size of hers, she could not.

Even though she was happy in her body, things did not always turn out so well for Évangeline's brain. She struggled to retain more than three lines of a poem and was completely unable to remember her times tables. Mumbling, she told people she was from 'Gua'loupe'. But if she sensed kindness in her listener she expressed herself with an exquisite charm and sweetness in the accent of Creole people. Mademoiselle had a soft spot for her – she was resitting the year for the second time – and congratulated her excessively whenever she answered, more or less at random, a question that only required common sense. Évangeline always had, hidden in her school bag, a big bag of sweets that she would pop into her mouth by the handful as soon as Mademoiselle left the room. She would offer them round the class, and a wave of giggling would erupt when Mademoiselle came back and, knowing full well what was going on, asked her, 'Nine times nine?' The answer was inaudible as Évangeline burst out laughing, spitting sweets and disarming Mademoiselle who could only stand, waiting, arms by her sides.

Teddy had been the pet of the girl from Gua'loupe from the first term he arrived. She waited for him at the entrance, kissed him on both cheeks, and hugged him to her bosom with a possessive tenderness. When there were witnesses he squirmed, but if they were alone he let her hold his head and snuggle it between her breasts, where a gold cross glinted and he was scratched by something furry which turned out to be a rabbit's paw mounted on a piece of horn. Évangeline smelt of vanilla, a smell that was easy to identify for a boy who loved ice-cream cornets. Usually she came to school and went home to Rue de la Pompe on her own, stuffing herself all the way with cakes and ice creams at every *pâtisserie*, but occasionally her father came to collect her when school finished. It would have been hard to imagine a man more different: tall, slender, with slicked-down hair and a pencil moustache, sitting nonchalantly at the wheel of a cream-coloured open tourer. His complexion was perfectly white and he smoked cigars. According to Évangeline, her mother could not stand the cold and preferred to stay behind in Guadeloupe; she was apparently nearly white and waited on by servants who were much blacker than she was, in a big house by the Caribbean. At Mademoiselle de Cordemoy's Évangeline was in clover, surrounded by admirers who loved her giggles and gaiety and the massive goodness that radiated from her. No one would have dreamt of making fun of her size or the colour of her skin or her laziness. It was probable that she didn't learn anything quite deliberately, so that she could stay in the same class, whose pupils changed every year.

Teddy was torn between two loves, one for Évangeline, wild and exotic, and another, unreciprocated, for Huguette, the girl who sat on his right. If you were to open Évangeline up like a Russian doll, you could fit half a dozen Huguettes inside her. One was as mute and diligent as the other was exuberant and warm. Huguette was the best pupil at the school, yet one day Mademoiselle still felt the need to say to her mother, 'It's even more commendable, what with her being so beautiful.' This is a good example of how education has a fixed idea that success in examinations is incompatible with a certain kind of physical appearance or, worse still, with sporting ability. Overhearing these words at the school gate from the lips of an excellent teacher, Blanche repeated them at dinner that evening, sparking a sarcastic response from Papa.

'On that basis, Mademoiselle de Cordemoy must always have come top in class without any merit at all.'

Teddy himself did not think there was anything incompatible between Huguette's bone-china looks and her keenness to study. He just wanted her to ignore him a bit less. Whenever she bent over her exercise book, pen poised, for a dictation, Teddy would steal sidelong glances. A blond fringe covered her forehead, her nose was unbelievably delicate, and she had an exquisite mouth. Her hands were so lovely that he was amazed to find out she was already a talented pianist. On top of all this, in contrast to Évangeline, who came to school dressed either in ruby red, canary yellow or electric blue, Huguette's outfits were a model of elegant discretion: pastel-coloured dresses, white or blue smocks, and in winter neat tweed suits.

At the end of the day, when the last rays of sunlight stole through the half-obscured windows, Huguette's profile was so delicate and her skin so translucent that she seemed not to be alive but instead to be a piece of Dresden china, poised to listen to Mademoiselle or write down a precept of grammar in her exercise book. She did not shake hands, and she held herself so stiffly that it was out of the question to kiss her on the cheek when he arrived or left. Teddy nevertheless felt an odd uncertainty about her, the source of which he could not pin down, but the burning memory of which remained intact. Huguette led a double life. She had a mother who was her absolute opposite. Shortly before four o'clock, the whole class began to listen out for the sound of a motor-car engine that made the windows rattle. A nudge of the throttle revved it before the driver switched off the ignition. Huguette put away her pen and pencil (she was the only one who owned a galalith pen) and ran for the door as soon as Mademoiselle dismissed them. Outside an Amilcar roadster with chequer-plate aluminium coachwork was waiting. Unless it was raining, Huguette's mother always drove with both hood and windscreen down, and she waited at the wheel for her daughter, smoking. She was the opposite of Blanche, who was always so elegant everyone thought she must have just come straight from the hairdresser's (people didn't say beautician yet). Madame D. instead sported an open aviator's jacket over a roll-neck sweater, mica goggles pushed up on her forehead, and a *béret basque* from which two kiss-curls escaped at her temples. Her lips were an aggressive violet. That this strange creature should be the mother of an elf like Huguette was a logical absurdity, but the little girl would nevertheless throw her school bag into the car, clamber over the door, flop into the bucket seat next to her mother, and the Amilcar would zoom away with a noise like a machine gun to disappear at the top of Avenue Mozart, leaving behind a pleasant smell of engine oil.

When school was over, a curtain fell on people's private lives. Almost as soon as Huguette dropped into the seat beside her mother she was no longer there for anyone, but gone without even a goodbye wave to Teddy and the others, vanishing into thin air, no more than a memory for those who had spent the day with her, exchanged a look or very occasionally a smile. And she was so perfect, it was hard even to summon up an image of her. You can't reconstitute, in the abstract, a creature conceived, composed and designed by God, then rashly entrusted to a whizz-bang Jason at the helm of her silver Argo, an Amilcar with chequer-plate aluminium coachwork and red-spoked wheels that threw out a disdainful plume of blue smoke whose smell lingered long after it had disappeared.

Teddy was finding out that there are some women so unreachable they are only present for the twinkling of an eye. Of course the same could not be said of Évangeline, who, as soon as Huguette had vanished, took possession of Teddy, pressing him against her, hugging him tightly, planting a wet kiss on his cheek and – the horror! – inserting a sharp tongue in his ear. 'Do you like it?' she asked. No, he did not like it, but when Huguette had gone he didn't care about anything any more. From the pavement they could hear Mademoiselle de Cordemoy opening the windows to blow away the smell of the little farts her pupils had accumulated during the day. Then a distant, hollow roaring would make her bang the casements shut again as she called out, 'I'm coming, I'm coming!'

Blanche, invariably a few minutes late, always had a kind word for Évangeline before scooping up her property and leading him away in the direction of Rue Henri-Heine.

At the back of their apartment his bedroom looked out over a garden. Already day was breaking, hesitant, still grey, oddly silent. Afraid to disturb his parents' rest, because they must have come back late from their Christmas Eve party and because, before they went, they had urged him not to get up till they came and fetched him, Teddy pulls the sheet and blankets over his head and, despite his impatience, persuades himself that the night is still dragging on. Of course he was mildly disappointed when he found out for certain that Father Christmas didn't exist, but he had simultaneously experienced a feeling of secret superiority over the children of his own age who naively went on believing in him. The apartment at Rue Henri-Heine had only one chimney, in the sitting room, and it was highly improbable that an old man with a white beard who was also rather stout and had his arms laden with presents and a sack stuffed with toys could get down it. The day this illusion was shattered, Teddy had crossed an invisible frontier. Fairies, wizards, witches and elves were left behind on the other side. From time to time a picture book he had forgotten at the bottom of a drawer reminded him, but they no longer interested him. He had cast off on his own voyages, plunged into thick forests, got lost in deep valleys filled with Indians and wild animals, nearly died of thirst in the desert and of cold in the polar wastes. He had made new friends: Robinson Crusoe, Mayne Reid's Plant Hunters, Long John Silver and his parrot. With them his adventures were without end, and the universe exploded, racing away in different directions, and the men he encountered there and whose heroic progress he followed were proud and brave. He left them behind at night when Blanche came to kiss him goodnight and turn his light off, and he rejoined them in the morning as he half slept, half dreamt before Papa came to get him out of bed.

But this morning there was no school at Mademoiselle de Cordemoy's. Évangeline had left for the Midi with her father (did she really have a mother?), Huguette was in the mountains with her mother (did she really have a father?), Paris was empty. And now suddenly the emptiness was filling with life and people: voices, laughter, footsteps in the hall. He half pushed his bedclothes off and pretended to be asleep as his mother opened his bedroom door.

'Come on, lazy boy! Merry Christmas!'

In her long silver dress her shoulders, which were very beautiful, were bare and dimpled; her hair bounced, waved and short; she had added a beauty spot to her cheek; and her necklace of (imitation) pearls went once round her neck before falling to her waist. She was a modern fairy ... but there were no fairies, ancient or modern. She brushed his hair, made him put on his slippers, and let him run through to the sitting room. A bottle of champagne in his hand, Papa was filling the glasses his guests were holding out. There were five or six of them, apparently full of life despite having stayed up all night, the men in dinner jackets, the women barely warmed by their fringed shawls. The one Teddy was particularly looking for, Pat Paterson, was there. Teddy adored Pat because he was a kind, jolly giant, smoked through a long amber cigarette holder, and most of all because he had a wooden leg like Long John Silver – not a peg leg exactly, but an invisible mechanical limb that made him roll his hips when he walked, leaning on a cane like the ones British Army officers carried when they led their infantry in an attack. Pat was a veteran of the Great War. He had been a friend of Arthur Cravan, the poet and boxer. He lived at Montparnasse with a woman who looked faintly terrifying at first meeting and who moved in all the artistic and bohemian circles: she had modelled for Van Dongen, Kisling and Pascin, who had all painted her portrait. She was known as La Monicci, she had a lovely sing-song Italian accent, and Papa said she was painted like a fairground and festooned with jewels so big they had to be false.

On this Christmas morning it was to Pat and La Monicci that Teddy owed the bicycle that was leaning carelessly against the mantelpiece. It had aluminium mudguards, a lamp, a chromed chainset, a bell and, along the frame, the glorious name of its manufacturer: Peugeot. Never in his wildest dreams having imagined this moment, Teddy was so excited that he threw himself at Pat, hugging his long legs and feeling through his trousers the famous articulated limb that he was known to take off and stand on the dinner table when a party got particularly wild. La Monicci had come up with something else as well: a complete set of lead soldiers, Napoleon's general staff flanked by the Mamelukes of the Imperial Guard.

'My hereditary enemy!' Pat said in his picturesque English accent.

Teddy knew more or less who Napoleon was – the man who slept beneath the dome of Les Invalides – but he did not know that his friend Pat was a distant relation of Wellington. Anyway ... it hardly mattered this morning, when his

27

new Peugeot bicycle filled all his thoughts. He felt almost suffocated with happiness as he unwrapped his other presents, which, apart from some books, hardly interested him. His bicycle, with its pale-green frame with black stripes and all its shiny new accessories, put everything else in the shade.

It was a moment when Teddy badly wanted Maman to be there, to share an excitement so intense that he felt it was the best day of his life.

But she was in the kitchen, making coffee, and she was not alone. Behind her, pressed to her back, is a man with curly blond hair whom he has never seen before, and this stranger has his arms wrapped around her waist and is nibbling the nape of her neck. She is laughing, not resisting, murmuring words that could just as easily be 'yes, yes' or 'no, no', before she finally turns and sees Teddy standing tensely in the doorway, his eyes wide. She pushes the curly-haired man away. He takes a moment to understand, then, seeing the boy, detaches himself with a shrug of the shoulders. From the sitting room comes the loud laughter of La Monicci and Paterson. Mother and son's eyes meet. Blanche puts a finger to her lips. Their pact is sealed for life. No one will ever mention this, not now or in the future. Not a word.

And by doing so she cuts him off from his other parent, his father who pretends to know nothing or perhaps really doesn't know anything, thanks to a divine gift that is reserved for the most simple hearts. Let us not criticise a mother who feels an overwhelming need for an accomplice she can trust with her secret when she feels that she's bored or in love. But from now on, Teddy can only see in his father a man he hides from in order to avoid the Truth. As a result, their relationship will remain difficult to the end, an end that comes much sooner than anyone imagined, the day those dark-suited, bareheaded men slide the coffin into the recess reserved for it in the columbarium, facing a sea bristling with the white sails of a regatta. That was May 1933. As the smell of the incense faded, a breeze filled the air with the scent of orange blossom.

'Not a word' was one of Blanche's cardinal rules, as it was for others. Any violation was severely punished. You only spoke freely to yourself or to a blank sheet of paper. Silence meant that tragedies were avoided. As were comedies. It was the price you paid.

For there to have been that image of the coffin sliding into the recess of the columbarium, the white sails of the regatta, and the breeze laden with orange blossom that gave death a taste of something celestial and blunted the sudden stinging sorrows and remorse for a remoteness that had clouded their last years, for that image – beneath a serene blue sky and in the presence of a bishop, a bored prince, and a clutch of officials contemplating how much time they were wasting – to have been engraved for ever on Teddy's memory, there had to have been another Papa, the exuberant Papa of five years before, a Papa completely unlike his usual closed self.

One evening he had taken his little boy on his knees and told him: 'We're leaving Paris, we're going to live abroad … well, not really abroad … we'll live, in a principality, with, as the name suggests, a prince! It's a country by the seaside. The sun shines every day. It never snows.'

'Even at Christmas time?'

'Well, maybe, once every fifty years.'

According to Papa, the prince was easy-going, big and tall, with short spiky hair, and dressed the way everyone else did. He had been a general in the French army. Teddy had been put down for the *lycée* in the old town, and they would live in an apartment in a block called 'Le Palais Rose'. Everything had been decided in secret. His Peugeot bicycle would be sent on later, even though cycling was not really the national sport in a principality that nestled at the foot of a mountain.

'We'll be starting a new life,' Papa said.

'Will Pat Paterson and La Monicci be coming too?'

'No, but they'll visit.'

No one mentioned Blanche's curly-haired friend.

The change was astonishing. Papa had an official car with a uniformed chauffeur to drive him, and Maman was given a convertible coupé as a present. At home Papa's new aide Émile called Teddy 'Monsieur Édouard'. The cook, a huge Italian woman with a moustache, had the resounding name of Giuseppina Staffaroni. In the harbour were moored many yachts and huge cruisers that never went anywhere. From here Alain Gerbault had set out in *Firecrest* on his solo crossing of the Atlantic. The apartment's balcony looked out over the harbour entrance and its pair of lights, over the roof of a mysterious villa whose shutters were always closed. During the day Teddy would see men emerging in frock coats and top hats and women (always in twos) wearing long black dresses and pillbox hats with little veils that they peeled back to walk cautiously down the front steps.

They were, Papa said (one of his functions apparently being to know everything about everybody), Antoinists. They recognised St Anthony as the son of God and awaited his resurrection with acts of penitence and prayer. On the left of this building was another, which would have been completely unremarkable if, on the second floor, there had not lived a silver-haired man and two very young ladies whose main source of pleasure, it seemed, was to wander about their

31

apartment in their underwear – or nothing at all – in between changing their dresses several times a day. Teddy had spotted them immediately and amused himself by watching them walk back and forth, stark naked, in front of the window while on the pavement below the Antoinist ladies went solemnly by, clutching with both hands – as if unbelievers were about to snatch them away – their voluminous black cloth bags. A bit further up the street, towards the Jardin Exotique, stood a singular house at the edge of the boulevard, a palace out of the *Thousand and One Nights* with a façade of blue and green tiles encrusted with coloured glass. Lowered blinds blanked out its windows. This was the residence of the Persian ambassador, Prince Reza Mirza Khan. Blanche took Teddy there one day. The ambassador's wife received them alone in a drawing room lit by low lamps. As at Madame N.'s, scented oils burnt on a table. The lady seemed enormous to Teddy, but he was possibly confusing her with the jumble of cushions that lay squashed by her weight all around her. It was easy to see that, despite the puffiness of her face, she had once been a beauty. She spoke warbling French. A majestic mane of hennaed hair framed her face and fat cheeks, which were undeniably olive despite her concealing herself determinedly from the sun whose rays, filtered by the slats of the blinds, sliced her into light and dark stripes. Bonbons and cubes of Turkish delight filled a large opal cup that stood within reach of her blue- and sepia-tattooed fingers, which she plunged negligently into it to scoop sweetmeats into her greedy, heavily lipsticked mouth. Her sticky index finger and thumb had glued together the pages of the magazines and books lying around her, which she read avidly. Their unofficial visit was coming to an end when the ambassador arrived, a small man with a sallow face whose hair and moustache were so black they must have been carefully dyed each morning. As ambassador to a principality that otherwise possessed only the odd consul from those countries in its immediate vicinity, with the lightest of duties – Persians being thin on the ground, and the Shah himself having probably forgotten he had appointed an emissary to this toy state – Mirza Khan's chief value was as an asset to the roulette and *trente et quarante* tables and as a generous admirer of the corps de ballet. A dignified descendant of a great civilisation that had lost its way in the modern era, he bent over Teddy.

'What is your passion, dear child?'

Teddy did not have passions yet, or if he did, they were fads soon to be replaced by others. Blanche came to his rescue.

'He loves books.'

It was true, although it would never have occurred to him. Two days later a large parcel arrived that was addressed to him: three books by Jules Verne, in the Hetzel edition. It was a beginning.

It took him months to discover the principality. An enclave nestled beneath a mountain and lapped by the sea, it was a genuine reservation, like the territories provided for Native Americans in the USA. A community lived there, left home and came back at regular times, in accordance with a ritual that was always respected. At midday a cannon was fired, announcing the changing of the guard at the gates to the prince's palace. As handsome as tin soldiers, helmets bedecked in the white and red plumes of the national colours, the riflemen paraded across the square to entertain the tourists. Half an hour later, from the Hôtel de Paris, Berry Wall would emerge in a tweed suit in winter, raw silk in summer, white spats and gloves, a

33

beige bowler or a panama hat, a carnation in his buttonhole, walking stick in hand and sporting the impressive moustache of an English officer. Trotting along behind him came a chow that lifted its leg on the flower beds of a circular garden that people called 'le Fromage'. At one o'clock he sat down on the terrace at the Café de Lutèce, where he was invariably served the same dish, the same wine, the same brandy with his coffee. This avoided anyone saying anything unnecessary. At five o'clock he returned to have tea and toast at the same table, this time dressed in grey. In the evening he sat alone, in a dinner jacket, in the dining room of the Hôtel de Paris. When people greeted him, he would respond by raising his hat or nodding his head.

If the spectator happened to miss Berry Wall, there was another ritual. At 1 p.m. precisely a chauffeur-driven car would pull up outside the Hôtel de Paris. In the open cab were a black-gloved chauffeur and a liveried footman. In the passenger compartment, behind smoked-glass windows, sat an old man with a short white beard trimmed to a point. The hotel porters rushed forward with a wheelchair into which the footman would, with the sort of care reserved for a poorly dowager, help the old man, a frail creature in a coat with a sealskin collar, a muffler and a grey felt hat. In the lobby of the hotel people stepped respectfully aside, the men raising their hats, the women dipping in a sort of bow. A silence would fall as everyone followed him with their eyes as far as the lift, where the footman would turn the wheelchair fully around before the lift doors shut. Facing the onlookers, the old man would raise his felt hat with a trembling hand to greet them, or bless them, and the lift would bear the sickly invalid up, perhaps to heaven, if not to an apartment on the fourth floor.

Papa takes his son's hand and walks him towards the exit.

'Who's that man?' Teddy asks in a loud voice.

'Be quiet!'

This is a command he often hears. Once they are outside, Papa stops.

'Listen to me, Teddy, and never forget. That man, whom people bow down in front of, knighted by the King of England and Emperor of India, that man is a shark and a vulture. There isn't one dead man, one maimed war veteran like our dear friend Pat, whose fate has not paid him his commission. He sells guns and military equipment, and his name is Sir Basil Zaharoff. You're still a bit young to understand these things, but just remember: wherever you find misery and dead people, you'll find vultures enriching themselves.'

It was a lengthy speech for an eight-year-old boy to take in. It would not be forgotten.

On fine afternoons an old woman would come and sit on a bench in the part of the terraces below the casino that overlooked the clay-pigeon shoot and the sea. In an extravagant hat decorated with artificial flowers, her hands in fingerless gloves of embroidered gauze, she wore a black skirt that finished at her knees, revealing a pair of still shapely legs. If someone asked to photograph her, she would say, 'You may. I was Edward's mistress. You can't imagine how sweet he was to me.'

If anyone wanted to know more she would just nod, making the flowers stitched to the brim of her hat wobble. The toothless mouth, whose lipstick had bled a little at the corners, moved silently in contemplation of an invisible sceptre. She would raise her short veil, revealing a terribly wizened face that might have possessed a certain beauty in the days when

Edward VII had been Prince of Wales. On days when she was in a good mood, she would sometimes slide the hem of her skirt halfway up her thighs and kick her legs, saying, 'Who wouldn't go mad for a pair of pins like these?'

The Duke of Westminster, the richest man in England, walked past, a cigar clamped between his teeth, in an out-at-elbow suit with corkscrewing trousers and his jacket pockets stuffed with tokens he had forgotten to cash in on his way out of the gaming room. A woman walked a step ahead of him, not turning round. She had an imperious expression and a very mobile face and wore a boater with a black ribbon. She was dripping with jewellery.

Blanche said to her son, 'Look. That's Mademoiselle Chanel. Thanks to her we can cut our hair short without looking like servants.'

And how had the Grand Duke Dmitri Pavlovich escaped the massacre of the imperial family? He was there too, as proud as a grenadier of his regiment, drinking champagne for breakfast, holding open house for exiled Russians, and signing bills that the hotelier would settle from his own pocket.

Of the White Russians who lived in the principality and were selling off the last jewels they had saved from the debacle, there was one who had found a position that enabled him to remain the great man he had been before and during the First World War. This was General Peter Polovtsov, who ran the public relations for the casino and the private beaches. When he became friends with Papa and Blanche he showered them with signed photos that ended up pasted to the walls of

Teddy's bedroom. Teddy couldn't stop wondering about the pictures: was that handsome moustachioed giant, the one in the uniform of a Tartar general with a yataghan hanging from his belt, the same man as the suave host of the Sporting and the Beach? The same one who was served a tray of cakes for an hors d'œuvre, a second tray instead of the roast main course, and yet more cakes for dessert, and throughout was poured only vodka to drink? How – the question had to be asked – had he, on a diet like that, been able to scale the Karakoram Pass at an altitude of six thousand metres on a yak's back? And was he also the person who had been photographed in full dress uniform on a barracks square, inspecting rows of women at attention in their boots, tunics and helmets, their thrust-out chests bedecked with medals? Teddy had heard the general tell the story of how in 1917 in St Petersburg he had formed and commanded a regiment of women to fight the Germans. Their bravery had humiliated their male comrades and stopped entire battalions deserting.

His wife, Madame Polovtsov, was rarely seen during the day. She kept herself to herself in order to paint. Working in pastels, as a portraitist, her pictures, which she rarely exhibited, were disturbingly exact and disquietingly penetrating. Her best-known portrait was of Barbara Hutton, the world's richest woman.

'A sylph,' Papa said admiringly. 'When she's at home there has to be an attendant nearby at all times, making sure the doors and windows are kept shut to stop her flying away at the slightest gust of air.'

The news that this glacial, hieratic beauty, her face always shaded by a broad-brimmed hat and her body entirely swathed in silk, had commissioned a portrait from Madame Polovtsov had started a stampede of the Côte's most snobbish and wealthy inhabitants to her door. But Madame Polovtsov had turned them all down in her soft Russian voice that hardly rolled its r's.

'I'm just an amateur. I enjoy it … I enjoy it all too much.'

So when she suggested doing a portrait of Teddy, Papa and Blanche could hardly believe it. For two weeks of summer afternoons, then, Teddy is condemned to wear the same orange shirt and beige shorts and sit perfectly still on an uncomfortable chair. The only parts of him that are free to move are his eyes, which wander from the open window (with its restricted view of the Rock and the harbour entrance) to Madame Polovtsov in her white blouse, grey-blond hair held in place by a bandeau, sitting half turned away behind her easel. Almost from the first day, this person's noble features radiate such serenity that Teddy has barely taken his place on his chair, feeling faintly sullen at the idea of spending two hours immobilised and daydreaming, forbidden to give in to the all-round drowsiness of a summer afternoon, before he experiences a kind of pleasant giddiness at being alone with her. If she bends over her easel to fiddle with a detail, he can no longer see her and can relax and wriggle his hands, but the moment she reappears their eyes meet, and she smiles with a heartbreaking sweetness that wipes away every trace of the torments of her past life. Teddy knows from his parents what she had to endure before she succeeded in escaping from Russia with the general. She never speaks about it. Her pale eyes, which look as if her ordeals and sorrows have faded them, subdue the ten-year-old boy. In her serene face they are all he sees. Her lips are only just pink, her nose straight, her cheekbones slightly prominent. He feels he 'owns' Madame Polovtsov's face as much as she 'owns' his. The painter and her model are one creature from now on. After he has sat for an hour, there is a break. She stands up, goes and washes her hands, and comes back with a bowl filled with muscat grapes, and a glass of fruit juice. They nibble their snack together.

She asks, 'Have you got a girlfriend?'

Teddy is dumbstruck. Blanche would never ask him such a question. The very word 'girlfriend' conceals all sorts of forbidden words and gestures. Without giving himself away, he nevertheless answers, 'I haven't got a girlfriend, but I've got a special friend. She's called Katie.'

'Is that Katie H.? I know her, she's a tomboy. And do you want to marry her?'

'Me? Oh no! That's impossible. She's two years older than me.'

Madame Polovtsov, saying nothing, goes back to her easel. Teddy wants the floor to open up and swallow him. How could he have said something so stupid? And talking about age to this lady who is ageless, whose attractiveness is all in her crystalline silence and whose beauty is a gradual revelation, irradiating the drawing room where they are sitting and over a period of days, without his being aware of it, taking over his heart to the point where he feels despair welling up at the thought of the sittings coming to an end. How can he cope with this unbearable sadness that he carries around inside him and that will perhaps haunt him for the rest of his life? The worst thing is that, just when he would most like to be able to turn his back on her, he must bravely get through the sitting without melting with bliss at the light from Madame Polovtsov's blue eyes as she scrutinises him closely to correct an eyebrow or a strand of hair. Distracted, no longer of this world, she is utterly perfect as she knits her eyebrows, purses her lips, rubs out and redoes a reflection in his eye. A wrinkle appears on her brow and runs down to the base of her nose, between eyes of a blue so weak that when she turns towards the window she looks almost blind. Teddy overcomes his urge to call out to her that she must be very careful the sun doesn't make her lose her sight.

'Actually,' he says, 'two years between Katie and me isn't very much at all. When two people love each other, age doesn't matter.'

Madame Polovtsov does not react. She has a more important problem with Teddy's hands and asks him to separate them.

'Thank you. That's much better. Don't move for two or three minutes, and then I'll let you go, I promise you. It's the last time. If I have any second thoughts about a detail, I'll call your *maman* and I hope you won't mind coming back to pose for five minutes, no more. But I think I've finished.'

That's it … the curtain has come down, brutally, as it always does. He knew perfectly well that the blow was about to fall, at the precise moment when it would wound him the most. He grits his teeth and stands.

'You can kiss me,' she says. 'I hope you haven't been too bored. When I draw or paint I concentrate very hard and I won't have any noise, not even the sound of my own voice. One day, when we have time, we'll talk, you and I. A lot. Yes, a lot …'

He brushes her cheeks with a timid kiss and leaves without turning back.

Having exhibited the portrait in Paris and London, Madame Polovtsov presented it to Teddy's parents as a gift. The pastel drawing has survived the vicissitudes of war, migrations and house moves, and when Édouard looks at it today, it is not himself he sees (he has got used to all his other faces) sitting well-behaved on a chair facing the window open to the sea, the port and the bobbing boats. It is Madame Polovtsov who comes alive again in his mind's eye, her china complexion, her pale-blue gaze, the taste of muscat grapes, their skin bursting open between his teeth, and the memory of those first waves of unspeakable suffering that one somehow learns, one day, to associate with the idea of love.

Before we leave the White Russians, with their attacks of melancholy and terrible bouts of depression, there is one last specimen who Teddy often meets, at the bottom of the steep stairs that run down from the Observatoire district to the railway station. It is only a fifty-metre slope, but the gradient is as sheer as a ladder. The steps themselves are particularly narrow and high. An iron handrail in the middle runs from top to bottom. Because too often children have used the handrail to slide all the way down to the street and in the process have broken an arm or a leg – even in one case fracturing a skull – the practice of such acrobatics has been stopped by welding iron pegs to the rail. This was ill conceived, as it seriously underestimated the intense pleasure children take in doing things that are forbidden, especially those that involve grave risks. A new game replaced the old one: they called it 'two at a time' or 'four at a time'. The aim was to hurtle down the fifty metres and roughly two hundred steps by landing on as few of them as possible. The ringleader, N., was an Italian boy of about twelve years old, stocky and as muscular as a bodybuilder, with a stormy temperament and the thick slurring voice of a drunk. He hardly touched the ground as he flew from landing to landing, emitting Tarzan-like cries. Without quite possessing N.'s visual accuracy or reflexes, Teddy succeeded, by restricting himself to 'four at a time', in excelling at a speciality in which he had no rivals: on every second leap he would execute an aerial half-turn and so jump four steps without seeing the one he would land on (or not land on). After a few harmless falls, everyone had worked out their technique and the troupe – about ten of them every morning, before they went into lessons – would deploy its talents for the few spectators who appeared at the landings that led from the buildings bordering the terrifying steps.

For several weeks the show attracted a loyal fan, a tall man who, leaning with his elbows on the ledge at the foot of the steps, wore a suit of black shantung that had seen better days (N. was adamant he slept in it) and a white open- necked shirt. His swept-back hair was unkempt and he smoked one cigarette after another. More precisely, he would take three quick puffs in succession, throw the long unsmoked part away, then grind it furiously under his heel, his face screwed up as if he were exterminating a vicious insect. When he had been there for a while (you could measure how long by the heap of cigarettes piled at his feet), a tic would start up in his white face with its black eyes ringed with purple, his chin would lift, and two deep furrows would be inscribed in his brow. His luxuriant eyebrows were jet-black and his lips crimson, deep crimson.

N. said, 'He's Frankenstein.'

Not everyone agreed. Everyone had his idea of Frankenstein. It was hard to understand what the stranger said. His French was poor and he mumbled, with an accent so coarse that Teddy was immediately able to place it.

'Monsieur, are you Russian?'

'No more Russia! No more Russians!'

He pulled a handful of ancient sweets out of his pocket. N. and Teddy shook their heads, but others said yes and the sweets disappeared in a twinkling. Teddy knew a few words.

'*Bozhe, tsara xhrani!*'

The putative Frankenstein stamped his foot.

'No more God, no more tsar, no more Russia!'

A sudden wide smile, open and innocent, spread across his features and he held out his hand to N. and then to Teddy.

'You first, you second! You two boys very good.'

After this encounter they did not see Frankenstein for a week. A downpour flushed away the heap of cigarette butts that had accumulated where he usually sat. Had he gone back to deepest Russia? Papa, rarely for him, came home for lunch and, even rarer, had a sheaf of local and Paris newspapers under his arm that he read at the table. This was a serious breach of protocol. Between Teddy and his father rose the barrier of the *Excelsior*. Blanche, suspecting a scandal, did not dare say anything. Today the *Excelsior*, whose editorials by Maurice Colrat were frequently read aloud at table, had a back page made up entirely of photographs. Teddy's mouth fell open as he studied them.

'Maman, look, it's Frankenstein.'

'Who?' Papa asks.

'The man between the two policemen.'

'Yes, he does look a bit like Frankenstein.'

'It *is* him … the Russian man from the bottom of the steps.'

Gradually everything became clear. The crazed-looking man between the two policemen had just assassinated Monsieur Paul Doumer, the President of the French Republic, a fragile old man with a bushy white beard who always dressed in a frock coat, striped trousers and a top hat and went everywhere in an open car, flanked by mounted Republican Guards, saluting a crowd more amused than respectful. He launched warships, opened exhibitions, received foreign heads of state (always with identical republican courtesy), decorated brave policemen and firefighters. On 14 July the

French army filed past him for two very trying hours. He had to listen to the Marseillaise three hundred times a year, but that served him right for having wanted to be head of state and of course a moving symbol too, not to mention a slightly sickly one, of a country that had not yet got over the First World War and, for that matter, never would.

'Do you know this man?' Papa asked, holding out the page of photos of the Russian flanked by police and the President stretched out on a table, his shirt and beard bloodstained.

Teddy told the story of the competition and the man sitting at the bottom of the steps, smoking cigarettes and offering them sweets.

'What will they do to him?'

Papa said, 'I expect they'll cut this Monsieur Gorguloff's head off after a quick trial. I should think there'll also be an inquiry a bit closer to home to find out what he was plotting in the principality. You and your friend N. will be questioned and quite possibly put in prison. I shall come and visit you on Sundays with chocolate and Latin grammar tests.'

'Tip-top!' Teddy said.

For some time he had been falling in with his father's sarcastic sense of humour, partly to annoy Blanche, who disliked it, perhaps because she knew it was her husband's only way of retaliating, and now her son's too.

Teddy remained ignorant of who most of the characters were, but he watched the puppet theatre that took place around him increasingly closely. He would not forget it. The principality was a glass dome, beneath which a shrewd conservative had assembled the wrecks and refugees of a Europe devastated morally and physically by the turmoil of war between 1914 and

1918. At regular hours an invisible operator turned a handle, as though the country was a barrel organ, and the puppets took their places and played their parts with exemplary courtesy and faultless delivery. A touching, often ridiculous, grandeur had stopped the clocks, denying the existence of both the war and the post-war. Sheltered from the present, those who had been chosen to play a part – all survivors of that unimaginable disaster – were able to recreate the world into which they had been born before the great upheaval.

Just once a year there was a war. Floats and carriages festooned with flowers carried girls chosen for their looks – and from baskets full of roses and carnations they pelted the crowds massed on the pavements. Even allowing for the odd scratch from a rose thorn, it was far less dangerous than a mortar shell fired across no man's land. The style, the rococo of that era, was maintained in the hotels, restaurants and bars, right down to the smarter cafés. Mirrors whose silvering was flaking off reflected back (to those rash enough to look at themselves) fuzzy images like the plates the engraver rubs flat when printing is finished.

Luckily – because without them none of it would have made any sense – there was always an audience. You saw them straight away, flocks of visitors from another world – a world of no importance – disembarking from ferries floating outside the harbour and from trains and buses, and photographing and filming the changing of the guard and the celebrities and eccentrics. Without this attention, which the leading actors pretended to be unaware of, there would have been no spectacle at all.

Many decades later, a film called *The Truman Show* reminded Édouard of something. In it a television producer raises an abandoned child from birth. The child grows up beneath an opaque glass dome in an entirely virtual world. Special effects simulate sunshine, darkness, rain and snow, all to the rhythm of the seasons. Little Truman goes to school, where he's neither better nor worse than the other children, gets work in some office or other where his mediocrity is deemed perfectly adequate, gets married, gets a house and a mortgage, has children, is tempted by an extramarital affair, almost loses his job, and is caught in a storm on his sailing boat from which he is saved at the last moment. He never imagines that his life is being filmed without interruption twenty-four hours a day, and that the omnipresent cameras are transmitting the results around the globe to an audience that breathlessly follows every episode, as moral as can be, in the life of a very average citizen. Apart from the innocent Truman (read 'true man'), every other participant is an actor or an extra for life, acting with the predictability of an automaton, which is exactly what he or she is paid to do. When Truman suspects the deception and threatens to rebel, an invisible hand – a *deus ex machina* – pulls him back and places him back on the straight and narrow path of virtual reality, if one can use such an oxymoron. And so at all hours of the day and night TV viewers worldwide are invited to follow the on-screen happenings in Truman's life of utter nullity, as a paragon who suffers only vain temptations and minor mishaps in an ideal city where everything has been arranged to produce obligatory happiness. From this point it is easy to imagine that if suddenly the show's ratings were to waver (accompanied by a corresponding dip in publicity revenue), the cynical producer, wielding his godlike power, would have no hesitation in ending Truman's life (not without extracting as much lamentation from his audience as possible), thanks to a devastating cancer, a road accident or a random shooting by a homicidal paranoiac (the last a very American fatality).

Édouard recognised in the film – which was not especially successful, no doubt because it attacked the lie at the heart of the most powerful medium ever invented – something of the glass dome under which he had spent part of his own childhood. He too might never have broken free of it, if cruel events had not brought about his liberty.

They called him, if he was lucky – or even if he wasn't – l'abbé Tumaine, a laboured play on words that was attributed to the maths teacher, who was furiously anticlerical.[3] In fact he was merely Father Chomet, the chaplain at the *lycée* where he taught religious education. His classes were not compulsory and so, as there were often absentees, in order to collect enough pupils to justify his thankless calling, he would position himself at one minute to four in the corridor outside his classroom, a small room furnished with benches but no desks, a straw chair, and devotional pictures on the walls. As soon as the final bell rang, hordes of pupils would pour out of the classrooms and into the corridor, thrusting arms into sleeves, pulling on coats, shutting school bags.

The father was of substantial build. No boy preparing for confirmation escaped his eagle eye. When he spotted one hugging the wall in an attempt to slip away, or running with head down towards the gate, his arm would stretch out, far further than one would have thought possible, and catch him by the collar in mid-flight, the way one picks up a kitten, before propelling him unceremoniously into the classroom. As soon as Father Chomet had a dozen, he would close the door and note their names in an oilcloth-covered notebook which he would place with the missal in the large pocket of his cassock. A Hail Mary to start with, then on to practical questions. Each pupil had had his confirmation booklet signed by his parish priest the previous Sunday. The chaplain pouted with disgust at the sight of the signature of Father Ricci who officiated in Teddy's neighbourhood, a priest of skeletal thinness whose vestments had seen much better days. The chaplain was merciless: twelve Our Fathers, twelve Hail Marys written out legibly in a *new* exercise book if a boy's parents had decided to take their offspring skiing or swimming instead. The fear he inspired was far greater than might be imagined from his slender build and sloping shoulders. He had a neck like an ostrich. His face looked hairless, with rather curious rolls of flesh under his eyes and earlobes, shaped like droplets of oil. A dimple in the shape of a cross was imprinted on his chin below a tight-lipped mouth. To read or write, he perched a pince-nez on the end of his nose that left two ruddy spots when he put it away. When he took off his *cappello romano* he was vain enough to run a hand through his very wavy chestnut-grey hair. (It was a long time since priests had given up the tonsure.) His scrupulously maintained cassock finished halfway down his shins. He broke no rules in sporting, as his one luxury, silk socks with elegant low shoes that were impeccably polished – a million miles from the wretched clodhoppers Father Ricci wore. This Italian, with a face the colour of *papier d'Arménie* and a greenish cassock, was the black sheep of the principality's clergy, who felt he insulted them with his all-too-visible poverty. His mass, said in a yellowing chasuble that was too short, revealing his skinny legs in their holey stockings, was the only one where the congregation prayed with the celebrant.

'Father Ricci's exactly how I imagine the curé d'Ars to

look,' Blanche said. 'I'm quite sure they both wrestle with the devil every day.'

'No question of it,' Papa said, his face appearing over the top of his newspaper. 'And a fat chance the devil's got of beating Father Ricci the way he beats everyone else.'

It was well known that the chaplain had ambitions to be a canon. The prince's approval was needed, and he relied on his counsellors. The little beggars in his class were almost all children of distinguished Monégasques. The chaplain had to play a subtle game with them: to succeed in forcing some rudiments of the history of Christianity and of the meaning of the Gospels into their heads, and at the same time not to hurt the feelings of the most useless ones. His problem was his total lack of charisma. He was impossible to pin down. That wasn't true: for the adults his objective was clear; but for the children he was utterly impenetrable. Teddy's classmate, Georges G., repeated what he had overheard his father saying.

'That chaplain's as slippery as a bar of soap.'

The fact was that, on the one hand, he slipped through your fingers before you could work out whether he was being sincere or not, and, on the other, there emanated from him a smell (more than a scent) that announced his approach, hung about him like an aura, and after he had gone lingered, leaving behind something that felt like bad luck. This odour of scented soap seemed to fade gradually and vanish, but then reappeared mischievously when the priest, despairing at some idiotic response, raised his arms heavenwards or hid his face in his hands. Nor was he averse to displays of melodrama and, for instance, pacing vigorously up and down in front of the benches, hands nervously clasped behind his back, murmuring, 'We'll never make anything of you.'

The boys preparing for confirmation desired above all that nobody should make anything of them. Their gazes rooted to the floor, they did their best not to burst out laughing. Meanwhile the smell, halfway between lily of the valley and patchouli, left its trail as the chaplain passed in front of or between the benches. Noses wrinkled, quick grimaces appeared.

When Teddy reported this to Blanche she responded, 'He must be one of those obsessive washers. I've noticed it: there's something too clean about him. It hides something dirty. All the same, he smells a lot sweeter than your favourite, musty Father Ricci ...'

Musty? Teddy looked for an answer in the dictionary. As for Father Ricci, he's not interested in what anyone else says: Father Ricci is a saint.

'Poor Father, he just smells a bit too much of—'

Blanche stopped. Teddy would never know quite why his parents kept the Church at arm's length. No more than that: there was never any outright hostility, and they maintained with great firmness that Teddy should receive a religious education.

'Afterwards,' Papa said, 'he'll make his own mind up.'

About what? Apart from the Catholic Church, he can't particularly see who or what he should trust. At home there are friends who pass through: he has made a list of them. First is Salah Mahdi, a Moroccan with the looks of a prince, a Muslim married to an Orthodox Estonian. Hard on his heels is Georges-André W., a delightful slacker, an amateur magician, bohemian, Jewish. Followed by a respectable number of Protestants, a Copt and several freethinkers. But it's still a lot simpler to associate with those that chance has chosen. All the more so because his school friends preparing for confirmation, however unreflective they might be generally, are starting to ask themselves questions about their religion. As personified by the chaplain, for example, it seems harsh, punishing far more than it forgives. They have never heard him utter the word 'love', which the wretched Father Ricci, officiating in his shabby church (built but never finished by a dishonest contractor), pronounces often from the altar to his kneeling parishioners.

'May Jessous's love go with you!'

The difference between the two is acute. They talk about different masters. Can divinity have two faces? Can Father Chomet speak in the name of the God of retribution while Father Ricci speaks in the name of the God of earthly love? How can this dichotomy of divine representation be explained in the framework of the catechism, whose very first lesson defines Christianity as a monotheistic religion? One episode in scripture particularly troubles Teddy: at the order of Yahweh, Abraham prepares to sacrifice his son Isaac. As he raises his arm to carry out the deed, Yahweh stops him. Or so it is said. How can the God of love amuse himself with such a cruel game?

'Papa, would you sacrifice me if God asked you to?'

'No, my lovely boy, I would sacrifice God instead, after making him admit his responsibility for the ridiculous mess the world is in.'

'So would God be willing to do the same to us, to make sure we really love him?'

'I don't think so, Teddy. But ever since the world was created it has been suffering from a duality whose attraction is, to say the least, a bit mixed, and which is also leading it straight towards apocalypse, by which I mean the next revolution. We haven't got to that point yet, and our only recourse, philosophically speaking, can be summed up in two words: *carpe diem*.'

Teddy was none the wiser as a result of this conversation. A doubt had nevertheless been sown. The chaplain's words were no longer the voice of heaven. Conflict was brewing. It burst into the open the following Monday. Father Chomet grilled him with insincere goodwill.

'How did you start your week, my boy?'

'Not very well, Father. This morning I put my left sock on inside out and I immediately knew it was going to bring me bad luck.'

The class laughed. The chaplain managed a condescending smile.

'… then I knocked over my bowl at breakfast and I was late for Monsieur Pollack's class and he gave me a poem by Lamartine to learn by heart for tomorrow. Lamartine's so boring—'

'Very good, I sympathise with your feelings about Lamartine being "boring", as you say, but I'm talking about yesterday, Sunday.'

'The week doesn't start on Sunday.'

'Dear child, that certainly is the day it starts.'

'How can it? If there's a God, which is not as certain as all that—'

'What do you mean, *if* there's a God—'

Teddy had been speaking with his eyes closed and did not see the priest's face suddenly turn pale or his friends, who a few seconds earlier had been wriggling on their benches, now sitting stock-still, waiting for the eruption.

'If there's a God,' Teddy went on, 'I don't understand how he could have worked at making the world on a holiday. On Sunday God rested after he'd worked for the whole week, which therefore starts on Monday. And if I was God, I'd have spent some time thinking about what I was doing before I created the light and the air and the fire and the water and the birds and our grandparents and Adam and Eve and all the rest of it.'

Teddy had discovered the intoxicating feeling of speaking without fear, of taking on and repeating the disenchanted words and phrases of his father and his freethinking friends.

'… really it's completely normal, whether he's God or not, to have a rest, even though, like Papa says, it was a rush job and a bit botched really …'

The whole class had fallen utterly silent in their rows on the benches. But the chaplain did not explode as might have been expected. He was, instead, waxen, his hands clasped, squeezing his fingers together so tightly that his knuckles were white.

'Édouard, I would be grateful if you would collect your things, walk from this classroom, and from now on never think of yourself as my pupil again. I am afraid that you are no longer worthy to receive the sacrament.'

'I don't mind, Father; I'll ask Father Ricci to give it to me instead.'

The priest's outstretched arm – Virtue expelling Calumny – pointed at the door, the corridor, the street, the principality, perhaps the whole of France, the realm of the damned even.

That evening Blanche received a letter, which she immediately gave to Papa to read. From his expression he was not happy, and did not hide the fact.

'I've warned you time and again,' Blanche said, 'that you speak too freely with Teddy.'

He agreed, admitting that there was nothing for it: Teddy would have to go to Father Chomet and make his apologies.

Blanche picked up the phone and rang the chaplain. A female voice (though not very female) answered, 'Yes, *we* know. Édouard may come tomorrow morning at ten o'clock.'

A tall, bony woman answered the door. She had rolled up the sleeves of her blouse and was wearing a blue apron that looked as if it was wet through. Her hair was pushed up into a hairnet, and Teddy noticed that the shadow of a moustache darkened her upper lip. But the most noticeable thing about her was that she smelt strongly of Father Chomet's scented soap.

'Oh, you're the one who's come to apologise …'

Blanche had told him, drilling it into him: 'Don't say you're apologising, say you've come to ask the priest to forgive you.'

He corrected her. The 'housekeeper' was above such subtleties.

'Come in, I'll let him know you're here.'

She strode quickly away and stopped at a glazed door. When she opened it, Teddy saw a bathroom and a blurred form in a bathtub. The housekeeper came back, drying her hands on a towel.

'*Monsieur l'abbé* is having his bath. He says it's all right, you're forgiven.'

Teddy recounted the visit to his parents, not omitting the housekeeper and the horrible smell of scented soap.

55

Papa could not help laughing. Blanche was indignant.

'Did you know?'

'Oh, the world's much too small for some things not to be known.'

'And we entrust him with our children?'

'They're no angels either. I'd rather like to meet this chaplain. Man to man, I'll bet he's much more easy-going.'

A meeting was arranged at the *lycée*'s chapel for the following Monday, after the confirmation class. Father and son held hands. The priest, not very sure why they had come, opened the attack.

'Édouard was rude.'

'*Monsieur l'abbé*, I believe that matter is over and done with. Édouard came to ask your forgiveness. You were having your bath and, as I understand matters, your housekeeper passed on the message. You were generous enough to forgive Édouard for a misdemeanour the implications of which I'm certain he was unaware of. What makes me most happy about meeting you now is that it gives me the chance to say that I am really the one responsible for my son's free thoughts. He's rather too good at listening to adult conversations for a boy of his age, and he remembers the words more than the spirit in which they're said. I, and a number of my friends, happen to blaspheme rather lightly. We are not a good example for Teddy. He knows perfectly well that I have no faith, which is perhaps what has led me to become passionately interested in Renan ...'

The priest started. He had never expected this dreaded name to be mentioned, when the ostensible reason for the meeting had simply been Teddy's rude and sacrilegious comments.

'*Monsieur l'abbé*, Ernest Renan is not the devil himself. Yes, he turned away from the sacraments, but all of his work is that of an exegete who has never abandoned the search for irrefutable reasons to believe. You must know the famous passage from *Memories of Childhood and Youth*. I always keep a copy with me in my wallet, and if you have no objection, I'd like to read you these few lines: "Merely because a lad from Paris can deflect with a joke beliefs from which the reasoning of a Pascal cannot succeed in disengaging itself does not mean that Gavroche is superior to Pascal. It has taken me, I freely admit, years of study to reach the conclusion that that funny little fellow came to straight away. Few people have the right not to believe in Catholicism, for the threads woven by theologians are strong and it is difficult to unstitch them … I sometimes reproach myself for having contributed to Monsieur Homais's victory over his parish priest. But what can one do? It is Monsieur Homais who is right. Without Monsieur Homais we would all be burnt alive—"'

'Monsieur, I don't understand what point you wish to make. The incident for which Édouard was responsible is closed.'

Papa assured him that he also considered it closed and that he had only come to say how much he shared the chaplain's feeling that children's souls were fragile organs of which their guardians, humble moralists all, could never take enough care.

'Having said that,' Papa added, when he and Teddy found themselves alone again, 'I grant you that the scented soap he uses is truly nauseating.'

How many mothers can resist the temptation to read a daughter's diary, to go through a son's letters? How many wives respect the privacy of their husband's chequebook and appointments diary? Blanche gave in to such temptations easily and, knowing perfectly well what she was doing, made sure she left no compromising traces. When she discovered a minor secret of Teddy's, the situation became complicated: anxious to be loved by him as much as she loved him, she was cowardly enough to give Papa the task of taking decisive action. Having extracted from the morning post an apparently salacious letter to her son from a holiday friend, Maurice L., Blanche suspected Teddy of replying in a similarly smutty way. She was wrong; and it was precisely because she was wrong – because Teddy detested anything vulgar and, even though he might have been curious, fled with a disgust that came close to making him physically sick from the experimenting that went on in the *lycée*'s toilets – that Maurice L. took, from afar, a perverted relish in making him feel uncomfortable. At the beach that August, for example, he had tricked Teddy into going into the bathing hut that his sister Laure used to change her swimming costume, then locked him in. At twelve or thirteen Laure's figure was beginning to develop: she had small breasts and a shadow of blond down between her legs. Used to her brother's pranks, she showed no surprise and, ignoring Teddy, dried herself with a big towel and put on a new, dry swimming costume, smiling at a dumbstruck Teddy. The reader will not be surprised that this image should have invaded the dreams of an only child, who had no sister to spy on through the bathroom keyhole. Laure had perhaps even enjoyed seeing herself so admired, at a safe distance. In any case, she had pretended to attach no importance to the episode in the few days before she and her brother went back to Paris. In his letters to Teddy afterwards Maurice carelessly described, with a gusto rare in a boy of his age, Laure's secrets and the supposed intimacies she enjoyed with Teddy's rivals at Scossa, the café on Place Victor-Hugo where the pimply flower of the sixteenth arrondissement would congregate after school for *cafés liégeois* or *diabolos menthe*. Rivals? Teddy didn't really see it that way. Laure was just, it seemed to him, deploying her charms, of which the most charming were her innocent laugh, like a cascade of silver bubbles, and her delicate careless gestures to push back the hair that fell forward and hid half her face whenever she leant over. Thinking about Laure long after the incident that brought their games to an end, Édouard wondered whether what was so attractive about her, much more than her physical appeal, wasn't a disarming naturalness, an innate way of being at ease everywhere, including in the bathing hut where her brother had locked her in, naked, with an admirer whose main reaction had been respect at his first glimpse of that precocious sketch of womanhood.

*

59

What the incriminating letter contained, he never found out. What remained engraved on his memory, however, was the scene with his father, whose aide was waiting for him at the *lycée*'s gates at lunchtime. 'The director is waiting for you at his office.' The office was on the other side of the square. The aide, Émile, was a sort of giant, in other words not really a giant, more an enormous mass of soft flesh that during the day sat behind a table on which he leant first with one elbow and then the other, his chin resting in the palm of his hand, his cow-like gaze staring into nothingness – a metaphysical nothingness, as Papa said – his job being, a variable number of times per day, to push a pad of paper and a pencil towards a visitor. His seated position exacerbated the stiffness in his legs, which carried with difficulty two huge, highly polished shoes.

The director was on the telephone when his son went into his office. He indicated to him to wait. The window looked out over the port, which was filled with yachts. Édouard remembered two details: outside, the Macumbers' yacht *Crusader*, back from Italy, was in the process of mooring stern-to and hard by the *Jeannette*, which had not left its berth for fifteen years; and inside, in the office, the door of the safe in which Papa kept his most precious files, along with a revolver and two pistols, was wide open, revealing a document folder in red morocco leather marked 'Special funds' and a smaller envelope with the words 'Teddy's bonds'. For the last two years half of Teddy's pocket money had gone towards buying him these bonds issued by the City of Paris; an asset that much later, at a time when he found himself extremely short of money as a student, he would try and fail to cash in: they were worthless. From which experience he conceived a lifelong disgust both for saving and for banks.

But let us stay in the present, as the father talks on the telephone, Teddy stares out of the window, and *Crusader* throws a mooring line ashore, grabbed immediately by two port workers, and slips carefully into the narrow space left by the *Jeannette* and a fine black schooner flying a Dutch flag, whose owner, a Falstaffian character with a ruddy complexion and a booming laugh, is another of his parents' friends. It was he who had given Blanche a pair of silver cufflinks bearing the initials 'IBF', the secret badge of those who called themselves members of the International Bar Fly society.

Papa replaced the receiver and his expression changed: his cheeks flushed, his lips pursed, and his gaze hardened in his sunburnt face, his broad brow crowned by his blue-black hair. He waved a letter at Teddy, who recognised Maurice L.'s handwriting.

'How can you call a dreadful boy like this your friend? I'm going to send this letter back to his father.'

'His father is dead.'

'His mother, then ... thank you for telling me ... I'm less surprised now that I know that ... But in any case I forbid you to see him again, or to write to him or his sister. No tennis for a month. Now go home and have your lunch.'

The phone rang at that moment, preventing Teddy from responding. But what would he have said? He carried on standing where he was, defenceless and exposed to the worst impulse men have: their visceral need to dominate the weakest. Yet Teddy knew his father was good, that he could show great waves of tenderness (quickly suppressed if his authority was threatened); but most of the time he seemed taken up by an indefinable 'somewhere else'. Affairs of state, however small the state might be, had enclosed him in a fortress from which nothing that could be communicated emerged. Or perhaps it would just take many years, until long after his death, and the discovery of a secret notebook that escaped Blanche's destructive rage, to understand that this man was suffering from a sorrow so great that he could not tell anyone. For some time, he had also been regularly prone to pressing his hand to his forehead as he struggled with terrible migraines, which were scoring his brow with its first wrinkles and encircling his burning gaze with tragic dark rings.

Teddy, not knowing whether he should stay or go, stretched out his hand to the safe and picked up the pistol. The magazine was loaded. All he had to do was cock the hammer. He aimed at the port outside the window. Papa threw down the receiver and grabbed his son's wrist, twisting the weapon downwards. The bullet lodged in the floor.

'My boy! Oh my lovely boy!'

He squeezed Teddy in his arms until he was almost suffocating.

They would never talk about it again, just as they never again talked about his lost friend and the delightful Laure, who both stopped writing eventually, tired of not getting any answer.

Blanche was late for lunch. Who had she been waiting with to find out the consequences of her rather dishonourable act? She was surprised to see how calm her two men were, although her husband's hands were still trembling. All her powers of seduction would be needed to regain her son's love. But the practice of seduction was nevertheless a form of love: the love of being loved. By no means the most insignificant one.

Katie, Madame Polovtsov's only rival, was a strong, good-looking, slightly plump girl. At twelve years old she looked at least fourteen, and at fourteen people took her for sixteen, sometimes more. In a way it was a shame that her intellect had not developed at the same rate, but in other ways the discrepancy reinforced her attractions, to which her mother's friends (or lovers) seemed particularly susceptible. The minute she walked out of the gates of the Cours des Dames de Saint-Maur, gentlemen greeted her. Their keenness was understandable: the white socks, the knees revealed by the short pleated skirt, the blue blazer and the felt school hat with a rolled brim were more than enough to attract attention, even if her green eyes, fleshy mouth, a little blemish over her left eyelid, and her cropped hair made her no match for her mother, Madame H.

Everything would have been perfect if Katie (short for Katherine) had not, from a very young age, been in a state of fury at having been born a girl. So that no one was in any doubt whatsoever, she dragged her feet wherever she went, swaggered as much as possible, smoked eucalyptus cigarettes in the street, called her friends, including Teddy, 'old thing', and was occasionally seen kicking a tin can along the gutter and chewing gum. In Teddy she found a defender, an accomplice two years her junior, an equal who accepted her for what she was and enjoyed being with her more than with his classmates or any of the other, rather mannered girls he knew. In the summer the two of them swam at Larvotto, where one day Teddy bought her a *pissaladière* to make up for not getting into the boys' water-polo team. In the winter, whenever there was a film on that they were forbidden to see, they would secretly sneak into the Beausoleil cinema. Teddy would never forget a particular Roman epic in which the emperor's favourite, stark naked (although in those days no pubic hair was shown), was massaged by an enormous African woman. Fifteen years later he did not have the courage to tell a great star of the theatre, Edwige Feuillère, that he had seen her completely naked in her first film, long before *The Break of Noon* or *Eagle Rampant*. Another actress they saw was Betty Stockfeld: he would have liked to see more of her films. This curvy blonde Australian appeared regularly in French productions, in which her accent earned her a certain distinction, and on every occasion, whatever the script said, the director took particular pleasure in showing her in a bra and placing her on the edge of a bed where he would lecherously make her take off her stockings, or put them on. A scene that unfailingly slowed down the film, but had its aficionados. For the rest of his life Édouard would have a predilection for women with an English accent and a preference for stockings and suspenders over tights. Katie did not share his tastes, despite being English by her mother and French by her father, who had been killed in the war. Among the actors of the period, she loved Roland Toutain driving a Bugatti in *The Mystery of the Yellow Room* and Ramón Novarro on his chariot in *Ben-Hur*. These very different preferences made no difference to a friendship sealed by generous mutual concessions.

When the Beausoleil was showing a film without either

heroic or steamy qualities, Teddy would spend the afternoon at Katie's. She played the accordion. Her favourite tunes were 'The Last Rose of Summer' and Lucienne Boyer's hit, 'Parlez-moi d'amour'. Madame H., who had heard both songs quite often enough and regretted having let her daughter persuade her to buy an accordion, frequently suggested that they play cards instead. One day she had an appointment, and on her way out, wanting to give the children her instructions, she went into the lounge, where they were sitting cross-legged, playing cards.

'Katie, I can see your knickers!'

Her tone was sharp enough for Katie to close her legs immediately.

When Madame H. had left Teddy said, with genuine concern and perhaps equally genuine mischief, 'What's so wrong with your knickers that you can't show them?'

Katie thought about this, then agreed that, if the sight of her knickers was the reason for her mother's disapproval, the best thing would be for her to take them off, which she did, and they carried on playing. In reality there was very little to see, no more than a shadow, but it was enough for Teddy to get an instant erection and lose the next hand. He made a strenuous effort to look away and won the next two hands. They were playing forfeits.

Katie said, 'Whatever you want!'

He had no idea, so she suggested showing him her breasts. As suggestions go, this was not as innocent as it might seem. She was fourteen, her breasts showed promise, and she was proud of them when, in the toilets at the Cours Saint-Maur, she compared them to her girlfriends'.

'But no touching!'

He promised. She unbuttoned her blouse. Teddy was

embarrassed. Statues he had seen in Paris and in public parks had taught him what to expect, but those were marble, standardised, unmoving, and they didn't make you want to stroke them at all, whereas these flowers, like pink carnations set in soft mounds that disappeared when Katie raised her arms and swelled again when she lowered them, danced harmoniously and were endowed with joyful life, even playful life, you might say. Teddy went home soon after this experience, feeling deeply thoughtful. As did Katie, but more about her own boldness.

Next day the storm broke. Madame H. knew everything and had phoned Blanche to tell her that Katie might well be a wanton hussy, but Teddy was a peeping Tom. How had she found out what had happened, and from whom? They had been alone in the apartment. No one, absolutely no one could see them, and of course neither of them had said anything. So how? There was nothing magic about it. In the building opposite, on the same floor, lived an elderly gossip who kept watch on everything that happened in the street and in the neighbouring apartments. She loathed Katie, who, each time she found herself being spied on, stood a big piece of cardboard on the windowsill with the word 'Bitch' (she wrote it 'Bich') on it in capital letters. Lately she had varied her choice of words and started writing, imperatively, 'Die'. The culprits had not closed the curtains because they had not planned any of it. Punishments came thick and fast: no more cinema, no more swimming at Larvotto, no more games of *belote*. They would meet in the street, and as they left the Cours or the *lycée*, and sometimes at friends' houses, but their mothers kept watch. They had discovered at a young age that no crime – was it a crime? — goes unpunished, especially if you're innocent. They would see each other again, infrequently, in Paris. But the magic had gone for ever.

Katie was married at eighteen, divorced at twenty. Wartime doesn't suit reunions. And time passes: fifteen years, twenty perhaps. One day, or rather one night, very nearly one morning, in Rue du Bac in that smoky bar where, standing proudly behind her counter Madame Blanche, her eyelashes black with kohl, Cupid's bow of a mouth pouting, welcomes the cream of Paris's nightlife, among them more often than not those writers Blondin, Vidalie, Marvier, Déon and from time to time Jean-Louis Curtis, all night owls terrified by the prospect of going home before dawn, a woman of around forty, dressed a bit carelessly but with an elegance that is not easily learnt, and perched on a stool that teeters along with her, is drinking a glass of white wine and repelling the wandering hand of a long-haired young man in overalls. The hard neon light accentuates a fatigue in her face that is not far from complete collapse; she is a stranger, a foreigner, adrift among the workers at *L'Officiel*, the journalists downing their last glass after the paper is put to bed, and Édouard, who, as he habitually does, lingers to get the better of an anxiety that on some evenings he is hard put to articulate.

'Teddy! Let me buy you a drink!'

Without the little blemish by her left eyebrow he would not have recognised her, much fatter as she is now, with her lovely green eyes clouded by alcohol and her voice husky from cigarette smoke. He is ashamed of himself and ashamed of a world that can wrong-foot his stubbornly boyish dreams and riddle them with nightmares. And because she sees him suddenly disconcerted, lost in thought at those scraps of the past and assailed by their images, she sits up straight and stops wobbling on her stool, and her face, by a kind of miracle, regains its youthful cheekiness, a sudden flash of saucy innocence, all its charming spontaneity. Or is it he who, in an irresistible rush, corrects with his memory the faded degraded portrait of a being whose decline he wants desperately to deny, whose image he so badly wants to save, a being he loved, even if she was loved with something other than love.

'Do you remember our last game of cards?' he says.

Does she ever! She smiles and starts to laugh, then, nearly choking with laughter, dabs a trickle of saliva from the edge of her lip where her lipstick has feathered, and shuts her eyes for an instant, as if she is about to fall asleep. Her eyelids are heavy with silver eyeshadow. Édouard moves between her and the over-friendly long-haired young man posing as the accursed artist, takes her by the arm and waist, and steers her towards the door and out of the smoke-filled bar. The room falls suddenly silent as they go. He guides her towards his open-topped sports car, folds her gently into the passenger seat, and brushes her forehead with a calming kiss. He drives carefully towards Passy, where day is breaking at last.

'I'd like to go for a drive around the Bois,' Katie says.

They drive as far as Longchamp and back via the lake and Ranelagh. The morning air has woken her up and she lights a cigarette.

'Let's go round again, can we?'

They retrace their steps. At the lakeside a man in a woolly hat is throwing bread to the gathered swans.

'He's there every morning. Shall we go back?'

At the door of her apartment, she says, 'That did me so much good. I'm not going to suggest I show you my tits again. You wouldn't believe what they look like now! You know ... that old bitch who told on us ... she died in a fire. Burnt to a crisp. There is some justice. If she hadn't done what she did, we might have stayed friends till the day we died. You might even have been my lover for ever. Goodbye, sweet Teddy. You can't know how wonderful it was for me to bump into you tonight, of all nights ... That's enough! No, no questions! Goodbye, sweet Teddy.'

Of the rest of the story, the vanished pages between the beginning and their meeting at the Bar-Bac, and between the Bar-Bac and the end, have never been found.

Teddy suffered from repeated throat infections. Vile beasts roamed and multiplied behind his uvula, robbing him of his voice and preventing him from swallowing anything except warm liquids. The advantage was that each attack confined him to the apartment, where he spent days in his dressing gown, his neck wrapped in a silk scarf, his throat stained with methylene blue. When both parents were out, he went straight to the forbidden books in his father's library. By the time he was twelve he had already read Francis Carco (*Perversity*), Maurice Dekobra (*The Madonna of the Sleeping Cars*), Marcelle Tinayre (*The House of Sin*), Maurice Magre (*Priscilla of Alexandria*), Renée Dunan (*The Jersey Silk Knickers*), Marcel Prévost of the Académie Française (*The Half-Virgins*), and several other novels whose names have sunk into oblivion.

When his sore throats proved persistent, he was taken to Nice to be seen by a well-known ear, nose and throat specialist. Dr V. was a handsome man, elegant and decisively authoritative. In his opinion a tonsillectomy was the answer: there was nothing simpler. Teddy would spend two days in the clinic. Papa, who had gone with him, used the occasion to mention the headaches he was having in the area of his left frontal lobe. The doctor examined the back of Papa's eye with a magnifying glass and an electric light, asked him to elaborate on his symptoms, and diagnosed common sinusitis. He suggested that, using a probe, he could scrape Papa's sinus, which was blocked with fluid. The two procedures could be carried out on the same day. Teddy and Papa would share a room on the first floor. An appointment was made for the following week. It was all organised at great speed, but Papa was convinced. As they drove home he told Teddy, 'We must put our faith in experts.'

Even allowing for the fact that this was the 1930s, the 'clinic' hardly resembled a genuine clinic. It was an old, grand private house, and when they arrived a male nurse led them to a bedroom with a four-poster bed and another bed – a camp bed – next to a double-width window with heavy curtains held back by gold tie-backs. The furniture was more than antique. The walls were covered in a tired damask fabric, and from his bed Teddy could study at length the engravings that had been hung on them: they were a series of illustrations from La Fontaine's *Fables*. He saw that Papa was taken aback by the room, which hardly conformed to the conventional image of a room in a clinic, an impression reinforced by the nurse, Auguste, who told them solemnly (not quite dabbing a tear from the corner of his eye) that the doctor's grandmother had died there a month ago.

'I can still feel her presence,' he added.

It was true that the room gave off a waxy smell, a lingering odour of infusions and unguents, and possibly even incontinence. Fortunately Papa was as much a practised exponent of the art of making unpleasant situations bearable as he was of expressing his pessimism about promising ones.

'Everything that might remind us that we're both about to

go under the knife is blotted out by this ugly bedroom,' he said. 'We've just come to spend a very brief weekend with some provincial relations instead.'

Dr V. arrived in his white coat. He wore his stethoscope the way others wore the broad sash of the Légion d'honneur. His self-confidence was contagious. Teddy and his father would eat a light dinner, and the procedures were arranged for eight o'clock and eight thirty the following morning.

'Above all, there's no need to worry,' he said as he left.

Papa, visibly offended, did not answer. Not long before, he had refused to let himself be anaesthetised for an operation on his elbow. He liked to tell the story of the Spartan boy who stole a fox and, hiding it under his tunic, let it eat his stomach rather than reveal the theft. Dinner was frugal and served by Auguste, who had put on a striped waistcoat for the occasion. Between the soup (disgusting) and the dessert (a biscuit of uncertain age) they found out that Auguste had spent ten years in the colonial infantry. As a medical orderly, he added, to justify his current role. He was a tall man with a handsome moustache, a crew cut and an Alsatian accent.

He gave both patients a pill to help them sleep, and the next morning Teddy struggled to open his eyes when Auguste brought him a glass of mineral water, which was all he was allowed for breakfast. He followed the nurse downstairs to the operating room in his pyjamas, with Papa's encouragement ringing in his ears. Papa himself had decided to take his time washing and getting ready.

'Operating theatre' was a flattering description of the big white room he was taken to. A number of details pointed to its having been the kitchen, now equipped with a sink, an autoclave, an almost empty pharmacist's cabinet and an operating table. Teddy was not asked to lie down. Auguste, in a tunic less white than it might have been, sat on a chair and instructed him to sit on his lap, where he wrapped him tightly in a sheet as though he was in a straitjacket. Dr V. had put on an odd round white cap that sat precariously on his head.

'Breathe very deeply into the mask and you'll go to sleep. Auguste will be holding his hand over your heart to make sure everything's all right. Don't be scared!'

Teddy was as cross as his father had been the previous evening.

'I'm very brave.'

'That's good!' Auguste said. 'You'll make a good soldier.'

Dr V. picked up from the table what looked like a pair of secateurs made of chromed steel. Teddy boldly filled his lungs with ether and instantly fell into a savage darkness, where men in white writhed and yelled. He woke up before it was over. A pair of pliers was still carving up his throat and he vomited a stream of blood onto the sheet he was wrapped in. It was over. He continued to vomit into a bowl, blood clots, lumps of something else that was foul and stinking; perhaps they were alive, perhaps they were those famous microbes with feet covered in tiny hairy hooks that had been marinating deep inside his throat for months. Auguste held the bowl firmly under Teddy's chin as it filled with blood and vomit, while Dr V. carefully put his tonsils in a bottle of alcohol, like two shrivelled kidneys, red and brown and greenish.

'There you are,' he said, 'guard them with your life and don't let them escape. They ruined your life, and if they get out they could climb back into your throat. Or your girlfriend's,' he added.

Teddy, outraged that the man should treat him like an idiot, could not think of anything to say. He was racked with spasms, and sweat poured off him. He had nothing left in his stomach to throw up. This was easily the worst part. Auguste released him from the straitjacket and tried to make him stand up, but realised he would have to carry him to his room.

Halfway up the stairs they met his father, in pyjamas.

'Did it hurt?'

Teddy shook his head and threw up into the towel that covered his mouth. In bed he went back to sleep, nauseated by a smell of ether that he couldn't get away from. He woke up when his father returned, pale and with a bloody plug of dressing in his left nostril. Papa leant over him and stroked his forehead.

'Maman's coming to visit this afternoon. Go to sleep.'

The drawn curtains plunged them into darkness. They were both too wounded to sleep deeply, and were kept awake by car horns, the calls of people passing in the street, a door that banged on the floor below. Teddy had waking dreams. His throat burnt as if someone was lighting a fire in it every time he swallowed some saliva. Papa slept, whistling gently, his wheezing muffled whenever his breathing got blocked. Hours passed. How many? Neither of them could have said. Blanche appeared, tiptoeing into the room. She smelt deliciously good, with that faint scent that followed her like a shadow from the moment she appeared in the morning and accompanied her poise and the slightest of her movements like background music. A bedside light went on. She opened a box of chocolates. Teddy shook his head. Her husband looked tenderly at her and said, 'He can't talk or eat, except for ice cream.'

'What about you?'

'Me? I'm extremely well! And I loathe chocolate, as you know.'

74

His face moved as he spoke and the dressing fell out of his nose. Blood ran into his mouth. Blanche looked frantically for a bell, couldn't find one, and ran out of the room. She came back with Auguste. There was nothing to be alarmed about. Everything was normal. Teddy would be served his ice cream, and Monsieur could have his dinner in bed. The nurse-attendant drew back the curtains. The sun was red in the late afternoon. Blanche opened the window and fresh air streamed into the room, chasing away the medicinal smells. There was a rattle of corrugated iron, followed by an altercation in dialect.

'Close it!' Papa said.

'But it smells disgusting!'

'Just close it!'

'It's better for resting,' Auguste said, shutting the window and drawing the curtains.

'What flavour ice cream do you want, Édouard?'

He started chanting like an ice-cream seller: 'Strawberry, vanilla, pistachio, lemon, chocolate.'

Teddy was unable to respond, except with a gurgle. Blanche knelt next to her son's bed and slipped her arm under his head. He opened his mouth and showed a tongue that was so bloody his mother began to panic.

'We must do something. Call Dr V. at once. This child isn't well.'

'Oh, the doctor can't do anything,' Auguste said authoritatively. 'Édouard woke up suddenly before the operation was over. The pliers slipped and cut his throat a little. Tomorrow you won't know it happened ... If you'd seen what happened last week, that was much worse ...'

Blanche became enraged.

'Did you hear, Paul? This Dr V., you swore by him ... He's a butcher. A fraud. You call this a room in a clinic? A mortuary, more like ...'

She did not know the story about the doctor's grandmother, but, gifted with flashes of super-lucidity, she had sensed in the ghastly bourgeois room a vengeful presence that intended to harm her son, and perhaps her husband too. Auguste came back with strawberry ice cream in a chipped bowl and Blanche slipped a spoon between Teddy's dry lips. But he couldn't taste the cold dessert: all he could feel was a blade of fire that seared his throat, slid down his gullet, and fell into a hollow stomach that sent a jet of strawberry back onto his pillow.

'Get Dr V. up here now.'

'Madame, the doctor has gone home. He won't be back till tomorrow morning.'

Blanche was so furious that Papa had to try to calm her from where he lay in bed.

'These reactions are perfectly normal. V. warned me. All we need is calm and quiet.'

'I see! Why not just tell me straight out that I'm not needed here.'

Tears welled in Blanche's eyes. They had never argued in front of Teddy. Since their quarrel – if it had been a quarrel – an extreme politeness had prevailed between them. In fact they had gone further, becoming attentive to each other in ways they would never have thought of before. This clash briefly lifted a corner of the veil, which was quickly smoothed back into place. Papa asked her to forgive him. Blanche dried her tears (two at the most) and her young face that was so lovely reappeared. Auguste, who had left at the first cross words, came back with clean pillowcases and sheets. Blanche helped him remake the beds. Papa was unsteady on his feet and had to sit in an armchair. Teddy let himself be carried back to bed like a parcel in Auguste's powerful arms and the nurse tucked him in carefully, threw the soiled bedclothes out onto the landing, refilled their water jugs, and made sure the curtains were closed. He said he would ask Dr V. to make an exception and call back to see them both that evening.

'There's no need,' Papa said. 'We already feel better.'

Blanche wanted to stay, even if it meant spending the night on a mattress on the floor. He dissuaded her. A good night's rest was the best remedy. They would both sleep. 'Won't we, my big boy?' Those words, 'my big boy', filled Teddy with inexpressible happiness. His father had never spoken to him like that before. In his happiness he tried again to swallow a spoonful of strawberry ice cream, and this time he kept it down and his throat stopped burning for a moment. Blanche decided that this was her doing and walked across to the mantelpiece to look at herself in the mirror. She dabbed her eyes with a handkerchief and checked her cropped hair that suited her so well.

'Well, my two men, I think I can leave you now.'

The early evening passed as they drowsed in the faint scent of the perfume Blanche had left behind. Papa breathed noisily and Teddy fought waves of nausea. Auguste came in at intervals to plump up their pillows and take their temperatures, which he noted on a sheet pinned to the door. Isolated noises reached them from outside: tyres squealing on the asphalt, a jammed alarm, the hours chiming on a nearby church. Papa had dinner on his own at a small table and Teddy swallowed another scoop of ice cream with difficulty. Auguste came back to clear away and freshen up their beds. It was only eight o'clock. It would be a long night. They kept a night light burning. Papa tried to read despite a dreadful migraine that aspirin – the only painkiller available at the so-called clinic – did nothing to remedy. He paced back and forth, pressing his hand to his forehead or holding his finger to the plug of cotton wool and gauze that had to be changed every two hours. Teddy followed him with his gaze and blurted out a few words. Papa stopped and bent over him.

'Does it hurt?'

Teddy shook his head and went back to sleep. He woke up again and saw that his father's bedside lamp was on and his father was sitting on the edge of the four-poster bed, a book in his hand, but he was not reading. The next thing he saw was the silhouette of his father at the foot of his bed, standing looking at him.

'Aren't you asleep, little one?'

Teddy shook his head. Papa put his hand on Teddy's bed and stroked his foot, which was sticking out from under the sheet.

'I treated you unfairly a month ago. I still think about that awful moment with my revolver ... fortunately God didn't want it to end in tragedy ... I'd punished you for something that wasn't your fault ... that letter from your friend. It's on my mind all the time. I hate unfairness, and towards you it's worse, it's a crime. My only excuse is that my migraines make me irritable, so I easily become unfair to you and your mother, and even to people at work, but there's no real excuse for being unfair to anybody. If you have children one day, never treat them unfairly. When you realise that you have, because you were in a bad mood, it's unbearable. My parents were simple people, and they hid their goodness by being very strict. I'm less simple than they were, partly thanks to your mother, and undoubtedly I'm less good than them too because of her. You need to try to understand me, and her.'

Teddy managed to articulate a weak 'yes'.

'... forget and forgive me ... so that I can be at peace again ...'

Teddy listened closely to the night voice, talking to him as if in a dream.

'... at peace! I only have one child, and then, in a ridiculous bad mood, I unfairly accuse him of doing something wrong. It weighs on my conscience, an intolerable weight. I need to admit all this to you, so that we can love each other again. After today we'll never talk about it any more. You must just try to remember it when I'm no longer here.'

He moved up to the head of the bed and knelt down next to Teddy, who was holding out his arms. Hugging each other, their cheeks pressed together, they wept and their tears mingled.

The boy would get his voice back, and the father would become distant once more, distracted again. Within a few weeks his sinusitis would turn out to be a brain tumour and he would be taken prisoner by another world, his turn to be aphasic, locked in, looking out with a burning stare. When they were alone together at the principality's hospital, where Teddy went every day between lessons, trying to get a reaction that would unite them again, his father's dark eyes, already dulled by the inescapable end, shone again for an instant, and the one hand that still functioned squeezed, lightly and repeatedly, his son's hand.

Each would have to carry, one to his grave, the other throughout his life, the sorrow and remorse of having so seldom and so inadequately said what they felt, of having walked past each other without seeing, of not having shown each other affection outside the daily social ritual.

The scars of an uncompleted childhood never heal.

On board her eight-metre *Aile III* Virginie Hériot aimed for the buoy below the casino and took three lengths from John Filler's *Glorious* just as the hearse, expected for the last quarter of an hour or more, stopped in front of the high Italian arcade that housed the cremation niches of the columbarium. The delay had been caused by the prince. The bishop had looked at his watch several times and made a number of murmured comments to his coadjutor. The choirboy responsible for swinging the censer was the youngest brother of N., the champion stair-jumper. Father Chomet had stayed away. The officials in black-bordered jackets, striped trousers and wing collars kept putting their hats on and taking them off again, not knowing which was right. The cemetery dominated the lower town, the Rock and Monte Carlo. The light was stunningly pure. To the east jutted the dark mass of Cap Martin, its red roofs half submerged in the green of the pine forest. To the west, Cap Ferrat slouched languorously in the sea. Blanche was surrounded by female friends. From time to time she lifted her black veil, revealing a face so shattered and pale she looked as though she was about to faint. The third person in her life had not had the nerve to show his face. Teddy was the only child present. Madame H. was there, without Katie. How he missed her! They would have nudged and whispered to each other. She would have cried more than him. *Glorious* had made up two lengths on *Aile III*. The prince, who was not fond of this sort of ceremony, finally arrived, wearing a coat and a grey hat, although he was known only to like caps. His presence was possibly an attempt to make amends: not once during the three months that his loyal counsellor had been in hospital had he visited him. Yet he owed him a great deal, if you believed Blanche. No one shook hands; people made do with a nod of the head. The coffin slid out of the hearse on rollers, and four pall-bearers placed it on two trestles. It was midday, the time when, if there was a dead calm, a breeze would blow down from the mountain and fill the yachts' sails. *Glorious* was attempting to pass *Aile III* to starboard and steal her wind. Hats in hand, the officials tried vainly to tame rebellious strands of hair. The bald were luckier. The prince was fortunate in having his hair cut short, *en brosse*. His hands clasped in front of him, stiffly at attention, he listened to the bishop giving absolution. The coffin was of oak, or perhaps it was a good imitation. On the lid was a simple wooden crucifix and a red cushion with the cross of the Légion d'honneur and the orders of St Charles and the crown of Italy. Papa had been proud of them. A modest vanity for a man who stayed in the background. A question hung over the crucifix. Would he have wanted it? He who, for reasons that were unclear, had implacably distanced himself from the Church? Wasn't there a chance that he would suddenly push open the coffin lid, sit up, and with an outstretched arm accuse Blanche, the bishop, the courtiers and his few colleagues who were present of having let him down? It was a futile hope ... Before they screwed down the lid he had looked utterly resigned; in fact he had looked … as if he was elsewhere, distracted as he had been so often for some time, and undoubtedly uncomfortable, bundled into his frock coat with his dress decorations pinned in a row across his chest. His stiff collar had bruised the loose skin of his neck, which had already turned a distinct yellow. Between the neighbouring gravestones and along the yew-lined avenues walked families awkwardly holding a pot of flowers or a bunch of chrysanthemums. The widows wore black, and the children were getting bored and playing hide-and-seek behind the headstones and mausoleums. The bishop passed the aspergillum to his followers. The prince shook Blanche's hand, then Teddy's, and strode away. Two stepladders permitted the pall-bearers to hoist the coffin up to the third row of the columbarium, where an open niche was waiting. The coffin was thrust into it. One last look at what was now no more than a box of polished wood, and already the niche was being screwed shut with a plate bearing the dates: 1889–1933.

'Édouard!' Blanche said.

Teddy too felt a terrible anxiety at the exact moment when the marble plate was being screwed into place. Had they made sure his father was dead, that there was no chance of him suddenly waking up in the darkness of that pitch-black chamber? If he called out for help, no one would hear him. To block out the thought Teddy looked away. A few steps from where he and Blanche were standing, three women dressed in black were walking past. The youngest was his age. The whole *lycée* fancied Lucienne: a beanpole in a skirt that stopped above her knees, with long legs sheathed in black. They exchanged one of those looks that postpone things to a later date. A bouquet of lilies of the sort that Papa liked, splendid, expressive and dignified, was placed at the foot of his niche. His faith in the benefits of the monarchy had been strong. Only her female friends now stood with Blanche. Not a single man. How could it be? She attracted men like moths to a flame. Could it be true that, in losing her husband, she had lost some of her desirability?

'Édouard!' she called again, more plaintively.

Oh no! She wasn't about to tell him off, was she? Lucienne had only distracted him for a second as she walked past. But a tacit agreement had been made, for four years from now, to meet in a carriage on the night train from Aix-en-Provence to Paris, the day they had sat their philosophy exam, but these were still imprecise matters about which neither of them knew the details. The prince had returned to his car. His departure dispersed the officials and the inquisitive. The victorious *Aile III* lay alongside Virginie Hériot's support schooner. Having turned into the wind to wait for the regatta's end, the white *Stella Polaris* rounded the Rock, its bow appearing, and slid slowly through the harbour entrance to tie up where the smaller ferries moored. To be called 'Édouard' in public was a novelty. There weren't enough cars for everybody. Édouard – since that was who he would be from now on – said he would walk, as it was barely a quarter of an hour from home. Marcelle C. said she preferred to walk too. She would go with him. She was a tall woman with very bright lipstick and jet-black cropped hair. People said she was Turkish. Papa used to say that she had the most beautiful legs in the world, and Teddy, as a dutiful pupil, had studied her famous legs on the beach and when she sat down and crossed them. From then on he had decided that they were the ideal legs, which they certainly were, or one ideal at any rate. Together, with her calling him *tu* and him calling her *vous*, and followed by two ladies who liked going to funerals and weeping, they walked back up towards Boulevard de l'Observatoire.

'I think,' Marcelle said with great gentleness, 'this is one of those moments when silence says everything we need to say.'

'Papa said you had the most beautiful legs in the world.'

Marcelle stopped. She put her hands over her face and shook with a violent sob, standing very straight in her black coat.

'Teddy, we share the same sorrow.'

She uncovered her face, which shone with tears that blurred her vision, but she was smiling.

'The most awful thing,' he said, 'is that Papa's on his own now. I should have stayed with him for a while. Now he's just surrounded by people he doesn't know who are prisoners too.'

Édouard himself was suffering from problems he couldn't admit to at that moment. His suit had shrunk at the cleaner's where it had been dyed for the funeral at twenty-four hours' notice and it was digging into him at the armholes. His discomfort had increased as he kept pace with Marcelle and was made worse because, as he had no black shoes of his own, Blanche had made him wear a pair that belonged to Papa. His feet swam in them and he feared he would lose them if he didn't keep his toes permanently tensed under the toecaps. His jerky walk was wrongly interpreted by Marcelle, who thought he must have been traumatised by the horror of the ceremony. He was certainly unhappy, but it was because at that moment he was distracted by an irrelevant physical pain that swirled around him, carrying him further away as each minute passed from the man who was now screwed into a drawer and had disappeared for ever from everyone who had known him.

'Marcelle, do you believe in reincarnation?'

Taken aback, she stopped dead and stared at him. All the innocence of this warm-hearted woman suddenly came to the surface: she had never thought of it, never imagined anything like it.

'What do you mean?'

'I read somewhere in Papa's library that when everyone who knew him on earth is dead, a good man is reborn in a child's body somewhere in the world ...'

'Well, that's not a very comforting idea,' Marcelle said. 'So we never see our loved ones again?'

If she was thinking about her own vanished lovers, she had reasons for missing them, despite never having felt any real attachment to any of them. With nostalgia's help we are very good at constructing false loves, heavily embellished by our imagination. They reached the apartment block where Blanche, accompanied by several of her friends, had already arrived.

'I don't know if I can go up to see Maman.'

'You can't leave her on her own. You're the man now.'

'My main problem is that I really need to change my shoes. Papa's shoes are making my feet hurt dreadfully. Otherwise ...'

'Otherwise?'

'I'd go and climb the mountains as far as La Turbie, as far as Mont Agel, and then maybe I'd come back in a hundred years' time.'

'Yes, well,' Marcelle said, 'that would be a very good way to get rid of your anger.'

*

They were there: half a dozen of them in the sitting room. Since Papa's aide had left, the cook, Giuseppina Staffaroni, had taken matters in hand. As soon as she was back from the cemetery, still in her Sunday best and with her hair covered by a mantilla, she had served vermouth and savoury biscuits. She was faintly surprised that she had not been invited to sit with the other women gathered around Blanche. She tottered in her stiletto heels, almost twisting her ankle repeatedly, and had never felt so divine. From the hall Édouard could hear his mother's exhausted voice.

'I think … I think that Teddy … I mean Édouard, now he's the man of the house, I think Édouard will be smart and sensitive.'

Marcelle's voice: 'He's been both for a long time.'

Another voice, probably Gladys F.'s: 'It must be traumatic to have to go from childhood to adulthood just like that.'

Afraid that they might go on talking about him, Édouard walked into the room. Sitting in a winged chair, Marcelle had stretched out her famous legs, now minus one admirer. The conversation stopped as he came in. Ladies sipped their vermouth. Gladys F. popped a savoury biscuit into her mouth. The crunching sound was so inappropriate that she paused and said emphatically, 'Dear Blanche, everything doesn't stop with death. You must face life bravely …'

And she quickly crunched the rest of her biscuit, which made a hellish noise that she tried to cover by coughing into her closed fist. Crumbs fell to the carpet and her foot, rather too elegantly shod in a crocodile stiletto, hid them by crushing them a little more.

Édouard left them and calmed himself by walking up and down the long corridor that led to the bedrooms, the kitchen and the pantry. No one had yet dared to clear the coat rack of cruel memories: a fawn overcoat, a Borsalino hat, a yachtsman's cap and a bamboo walking stick with an ivory handle. For three months their presence had shored up a fragile convention: that Papa would come back, that he had regained the power of speech, that he would go out for a stroll again, twirling his walking stick. His illness was a nightmare that would eventually end because everything was still in place including, on a small console table, his packet of rolling tobacco with which, after lunch, he would roll himself a cigarette in a Job paper. Today the convention had been exposed. It was pointless to go on maintaining the fiction that, against all logic, everyone had still clung to two days earlier. But who would dare to bring it to an end, and with what heartbreak? Édouard was finally able to take his shoes off. To walk on the tiled floor cooled his burning feet. The loose tile that crunched slightly was still there in front of Papa's bedroom. The door was open. Someone ... had put a bunch of anemones in a blue vase on his bedside table. His desk was waiting by the French window: the white glass inkstand, an ivory letter-opener, a blotter with his initials. The bed was made the way he liked it: two pillows laid on top of the bolster. The terrible neuralgia he had had in his final months had forced him to sleep practically sitting up. His carriage clock had stopped a short time after his departure, at twelve thirty. Night or day? Giuseppina Staffaroni opened the kitchen door and, crooking her index finger, beckoned him to join her.

'*Edoardo? Hai fame? Vieni! Ho qualche cosa per te ...*'

In the pantry, on the oilcloth that covered the table, a white cloth was draped over a round shape. Giuseppina lifted up the cloth: a tomato pie decorated with black olives and green peppers. She poured a glass of lemonade. How would he be able to swallow anything without throwing up, even if he was hungry? To forget he was hungry, he put his hands to his head and shut his eyes. The provocative picture of Lucienne in a skirt that was too short for her and black stockings immediately appeared.

'*Mangiare, Edoardo!*'

Giuseppina was extraordinary: a frizzy Gorgon's head under her mantilla, a swollen, lumpy nose, too much rouge on her cheeks, a coloured glass crucifix that dangled on a black ribbon from her neck, and enormous hands, their fingers deeply fissured from washing up, that lay flat on the table like a laundress's paddles. When she opened her mouth, a cloud of garlic filled the pantry. Édouard burst out sobbing and hid his head in his arms.

'*Non piangere, Edoardo! Papà è partito per il cielo.*'

Heaven! How far away that is! And the eternity of the journey ... as a prisoner of that awful box! Édouard at last lets his tears flood out, there in the pantry, in front of the pie and glass of lemonade, in front of Giuseppina Staffaroni, who speaks almost no French but understands everything, says nothing, and nods her head like a horse pestered by flies, making her heavy earrings sway fascinatingly, like a pendulum.

From the hall came the sound of muffled voices. People were talking as if there were a sick person asleep in the next room. Marcelle had given the mourners the signal to leave; their good intentions, and especially curiosity, were exasperating Blanche.

When Édouard went to find his mother, she was crouching in her bedroom in front of a mountain of letters, sheets of paper with handwriting on them, and small notebooks that had come out of a wide-open drawer in the Italian chest of drawers. After a quick glance – and sometimes without even looking, recognising the handwriting – she tore them up and stuffed the scraps into a canvas bag that Teddy recognised: it was Papa's sailing bag that he had used to carry a change of clothes, his wash bag, and two or three books whenever he went sailing.

'Will you leave me alone for a while, darling? We'll go out before dinner.'

She stayed in her room with the door shut for two hours. When she came out the bag was full to bursting and she had changed into a summer skirt and a pink shirt. Her hair was covered with a headscarf.

She said, to forestall a reproach it hadn't occurred to her son to make, 'What people will think of me doesn't bother me in the slightest. You change too, please. You look too sad in black. We're going to get some fresh air. We'll go for a drive, then have dinner in Nice or Cannes, somewhere a long way away. Take this bag downstairs for me and put it behind the car seats. If Giuseppina's still here, tell her to come and see me … Your eyes are awfully red.'

'I was crying with Giuseppina. I shouldn't have held it all back at the cemetery.'

'No, you did the right thing. With her it is all right to cry a lake of tears. She won't forget it, although you will. Now go and get ready.'

Night was falling. A string of twinkling lights picked out the shore. With her flags lit from stem to stern, the *Stella Polaris* was leaving port, her next stop Genoa. Worn out by their flying visit to the Oceanographic Museum and a stop at the casino where they had quickly been relieved of their dollars, the passengers were dressing for dinner, having a cocktail, or leaning their elbows on the stern rail and watching in silence as the harbour of this operetta-like principality, of which they had only seen the gilded stage but had had no time to peer into the wings, shrank into the dusk.

Sitting on a bench on the High Corniche, with the whole Riviera at their feet, Blanche and her son watched the fire as it consumed the last of the papers. The sailing bag had not completely burnt. It had burst as it caught fire. Small fibres writhed on the concrete, and every time a car passed close by on the steep road, pages that had turned to ashes blew and fluttered into the air. Calmly Blanche had taken the wheel and, without a word, had brought them to the crescent of ground that commanded this fine view by day and night. Édouard had hardly dared look at her as they sat together. She chain-smoked, stubbing out each cigarette with a sharp twist of her heel, nudging towards the last embers an envelope with a foreign stamp or the red oilcloth cover of a notebook that the heat had rippled like an accordion. At their feet the principality was a chequerboard of ochre roofs; rare squares showed where there were gardens. It was impossible to identify in this Lilliputian world the cemetery next to the hospital and the Jardin Exotique. Behind Blanche and Édouard stood Mont Agel with its canyons of holm oaks, scrawny olive trees and pines whose roots were dug into the scree left behind by ancient snow banks which his geography teacher said had disappeared in the last ice age, twenty thousand years ago. The earth had warmed up since then. Not enough: Blanche was shivering. Édouard went to fetch her shawl from the car to put it around her shoulders.

It was barely a month since his class, led by a young botanist, had come up here. From the north flank of the ridge a goat track wound down into the valley on treacherously loose stones. Gentians, mastic and Spanish broom grew on each side of the path. The botanist was crouching down to study a clump of saxifrage that had come up between the slabs of a one-time threshing floor when a hail of small stones started landing on him and his pupils. Higher up, protected by a granite wall, a group of shepherd boys had decided to defend their territory. They restrained their dogs, but not enough: one, a big slobbering mongrel, had bitten Georges G. on his calf. Not badly, as Édouard told his mother, but the problem was that Georges G. was aggressive.

'He pulled a stake out of the fencing and attacked the dog—'

'Mm,' Blanche said.

She had got as far as the hail of gravel, the stoning of one group of children by another, then lost interest.

'They're savages,' Édouard said.

'They're young men—'

'It's really near here. Just on the other side of the ridge.'

In five years Blanche had probably never seen the other side of the ridge, and it was possible she hadn't even been curious to do so. Ignorance was a blessing; another blessing was that mother and son knew each other so little. Night had fallen like a curtain. The *Stella Polaris* passed out of sight beyond Cap Martin.

'Are you still there?' Blanche asked with a catch in her throat.

'Yes.'

Their light-coloured clothing was all that showed where they were in the dark. Blanche would have liked to say things that could not be said, things that were beyond words. Inside her head, full of the sorrow of a woman brutally sidelined by the man who had once put her centre stage, what had just happened was simultaneously too fast and too confused.

'It's my fault,' she said in a low voice, 'and your father paid the price.'

When the cemetery worker had screwed the marble plate in place, hiding the coffin from them for good – oh, that cruel grinding sound of the screwdriver twisting into the marble – Blanche had stiffened, suddenly icy, separated for ever from the friends around her, defying if not their gazes then at least their private thoughts. She would not be judged that way! The only person who had the right to ask her for a full account had never done so. What arrogance on his part, and now he lay beyond her reach, locked in his coffin, entombed, and beginning the first night of his long road towards the ultimate peace of mind, leaning on his walking stick, its handle carved with a fleur-de-lys. Gone without a word, without the slightest loving gesture, overwhelming with his trust the only woman who had ever mattered to him. What an egotist!

She stamped on the last ashes with her foot. Acrid smoke made them both sneeze.

'Dying like that,' she said, 'is unforgivably selfish. What a revenge to take!'

She stood up and walked over to the car.

'I've got rid of everything,' she said. 'Make sure it's all properly burnt. I won't have to shed a single tear rereading a single letter your father wrote me, nor any that I wrote him.'

'Was it only your letters to each other?'

Blanche didn't answer. Of course she didn't. She was the supreme artist of the silence she then invited others to fill with their hypotheses. Édouard could put forward all the names he wanted to, some with certainty, others more tentatively, but tonight his mother was bulletproof, and the shadows added a mourning veil to her face, so much more beautiful when it was stripped of make-up, as it was now.

'Let's go to Nice for dinner! You and me! It's been so long since we did that.'

So long, Teddy couldn't remember it. Who was she trying to fool?

'It's a shame you can't drive.'

'I'm only thirteen.'

'Of course you are ... I haven't forgotten. I was joking.'

Joking? On a night like this?

Who had she been here with before? The *patron* suppressed a smile, took their order without resorting to the clowning he reserved for 'foreigners' and Parisians. The restaurant terraces overflowed onto the cobbles of the old town, filled with strolling tourists and people from the city's well-off districts. Passers-by studied the menus outside, little girls played hopscotch and half a dozen boys shared a bicycle between them. On rush-seated chairs outside old apartment buildings painted vermilion, ochre and yellow, matrons fanned themselves with bits of cardboard; plagued by rolls of fat at their waists, split by their enormous thighs, with their other hands they hoisted up, with index finger and thumb, the jelly-like mass of their breasts in blouses that were soaked with sweat. Up on the corniche Blanche had shivered. By the sea it was stifling. She had discarded her shawl. In her scoop-necked pink shirt she looked ten years younger and it irritated Édouard to see the number of looks she was getting. Brazenly young women strolled past the terrace once, twice, three times. Wearing espadrilles, they danced over the street's big cobbles on their boyfriends' arms, their legs naked and tanned.

'Look how happy everyone is!' Édouard said. 'And us so unhappy …'

'There will be moments, maybe no more than a few seconds, when you won't think about it. Tonight it's like that: no more than a few seconds. Tomorrow it'll be a minute, then in a while it'll be an hour, and in a few years' time it'll be days, months … But remember, whether it reassures you or not, you're only ever cured of the ones who leave you by leaving yourself.'

Driven by a sense of lost intimacy that he felt he had suddenly rediscovered, and because it was hard always to keep everything to yourself, Édouard confessed, 'This morning, when they were bringing Papa to us, I saw a girl I knew but who I've never spoken to. We smile when we see each other. She's really pretty; she's called Lucienne. At the *lycée* all the boys talk about her. She must be in mourning too. She was wearing black stockings.'

Blanche smiled, her attention distracted by an odd-looking man who was walking up and down in front of their table, greeting them each time by raising a grimy sailor's cap. He wore a striped black-and-white vest and a threadbare pair of canvas trousers that flapped around his legs. With a clipped beard and a pipe clamped between his teeth, he bore an undeniable resemblance to the sailor on packets of Player's cigarettes. The waiter served their hors d'œuvres and a jug of rosé wine and saw where Édouard was looking.

'He's never set foot on a boat. He looks after the beach at the Hôtel Ruhl. He can't even swim. If you buy him a drink, he'll tell you how he sculled all the way to Corsica, even to the Americas if he gets carried away.'

The main thing Édouard would remember about the dinner, during which he and his mother hardly spoke to one another, was a feeling of awful sorrow that gusted over him repeatedly and exploded in his chest. When it did, his heart stopped beating. An invisible hand gripped him by the throat and began to strangle him.

'Maman, I'm going to be sick—'

'NO!'

Ah, that short, sharp ... imperious no that gave him no opportunity to disobey orders, and no way out! Blanche was in control. She would teach him everything, by force if she had to, and with a gritty determination to avenge at all costs the insult fate had inflicted. She had hardly thought about this, but her mission suddenly exhilarated her. She passed Édouard a hundred-franc note under the table.

'Ask for the bill.'

When the waiter put the saucer down in front of her, Blanche pushed it towards her son.

'You glance at it to show that you're not a stupid tourist. If the tip isn't included, you do a quick sum in your head and calculate twelve per cent. If it's included, you leave a franc. Never, ever take the bill with you.'

First lesson.

The apartment was suffocating. Before she left Giuseppina Staffaroni had closed all the doors and windows. Blanche rushed to open everything wide and disperse the unpleasant smell of damp that so quickly seeped into the walls, curtains and carpets. In one of those visions that had been rare until now, but were destined to multiply gradually to the point where they were simply the outward signs of a universe in which she was a recluse who was sometimes inspired by God, sometimes by Evil, Blanche, holding her head in her hands, suddenly started shouting.

'I knew it, I knew it! *He* knew we were out so *he* came back here one last time, *he* touched everything and *he* didn't find a thing ... Because *we* burnt everything, didn't we, Édouard? But why did *he* leave without saying anything?'

In the bathroom and in the kitchen *he* had certainly turned off the taps the way he had once made sure of doing each evening. In the pantry *he* had covered the turtledoves' cage with a cloth, and on the library shelves she was certain that her book was missing.

'You see,' she said in front of the little console table, '*he* even took his packet of tobacco that smells so horrible. If he thinks he's going to be able to roll cigarettes for himself easily in that niche of his, he's very much mistaken.'

'Maman. Maman,' Édouard begged her.

Blanche raised her head and saw her son's eyes brimming with tears.

'I'm sorry ... I'm so sorry ... Do you remember those evenings when he used to come home a bit late? He was always anxious about you. "Is the little one asleep yet? I hope so," he used to say. We must put his mind at rest. It's been a difficult day for both of us, but we've done well, haven't we? Go to bed now.'

For Édouard it was a moment of intense confusion: his bed was not made, and the bedcovers were folded on the mattress, military-style. His table and chair were draped with a threadbare white sheet. He called his mother.

'Maman, what's happening? Don't I have my own room any more?'

'Oh, I forgot to tell you the good news. That room's much too small for a boy of your age. Giuseppina has made up the bed in your father's room for the two months we'll be here, before we go back to Paris. Then you'll be going to England to spend the summer with the W.s, who are so looking forward to seeing you. Try to sleep. I'll drive you to school in the morning.'

What time did she come into his room, without switching on the light, like a ghost in her white nightdress? Sliding her hands under the sheet where it covered his ankles, she grasped them and pulled them hard.

'Listen to me, Édouard ... and don't forget: I'VE NEVER LOVED ANYONE EXCEPT YOUR FATHER.'

By the time he had groped for the switch on his bedside light and managed to turn it on, she had gone. All that was left of her presence was a smell of perfume and the turmoil of her tormented body. Édouard had heard her speak at the exact moment when Papa, standing in front of him, his features hollow and his voice muffled, was saying over and over again, without getting an answer: 'Is the little one asleep yet? I hope so.'

Endnotes

1. The money from recycling silver paper was once given to help orphanages and religious missions in Asia.

2. *Mémoires d'un âne* by the Comtesse de Ségur.

3. A schoolboy joke that plays on the homophone '*la bête humaine*' meaning 'the beast in humanity'.

An extract from *The Great and the Good*

Per Augusta ad angusta

'You're going to Switzerland? You should go and see Augusta. She—'

The lights turn green, unleashing a flood of cars that drowns out Getulio's voice but fails to interrupt him.

'... recognise her immediately. Quite unchanged, in spite of—'

A cement mixer, its drum revolving as it chews gravel, slows in front of them.

'... still awfully attractive ... you know, I ... her grace ... her number ...'

He pulls a dog-eared visiting card from his coat pocket and reads out a Lugano phone number. Arthur tries to memorise it, unsure if he will remember it an hour from now.

'Excuse me, must dash,' Getulio says, raising an odd tweed hat perched on his sugarloaf-shaped skull.

The lights change again, and in three strides he is on the far side of Rue des Saints-Pères. From the opposite pavement he waves a white handkerchief over his head, as if a train was already bearing Arthur away to Switzerland and Ticino. A bus drives between them. When it has passed, the Brazilian has gone, leaving Arthur alone with a phone number that has been so long coming, he isn't sure he actually wants it any more. Especially not from Getulio.

*

As Arthur walks up Rue des Saints-Pères towards Boulevard Saint-Germain, his mind elsewhere (though not without looking back, half hoping Getulio will reappear behind him and carry on talking about Augusta), the phone number etches itself on his memory and he feels his chest gripped with anxiety. But why? To whom can he say, 'It's too late, too much time has passed. There's no use reopening old wounds'? Not the hurrying Left Bank pedestrians, or the medical students queuing outside a pâtisserie who force him to step off the pavement, which he does, without looking out for traffic. A car brushes past him and its driver yells a volley of insults that make the students giggle. To get himself run over and killed . . . that would be bitterly ironic, wouldn't it, twenty years later, when he would have done much better to have died back then, so that he didn't have to drag around the burden of a failure that still haunts him as an adult, even now.

He makes his way into the restaurant where two signatories from a German bank are expecting him. He likes business: it has taught him how to lie and dissimulate. Bit by bit, a sort of double has been born inside him, a made-up character who serves him remarkably well in his negotiations: a man of few words and a dry manner, who affects a careless inattentiveness while not missing a word of what's being said, a sober figure, a non-smoker who, in the American style, takes his jacket off to talk in his shirtsleeves, always has a cup of coffee to hand, and switches to first-name terms the moment the deal looks done. 'That's not me. It's not me!' he says to himself, if he happens to catch sight of himself in a mirror behind the table where he's sitting. But that 'me', his real self, is fading by the day. Does it still exist? If it does, it lies years behind him, a heap of fragments mixed up with the love affairs and illusions of his twenties. And if, very occasionally, in the heat of telling himself yet another lie, that self happens to rise from the ashes, it still carries the scent of Augusta.

The Foundling Boy

Michel Déon

translated from the French by Julian Evans

It is 1919. On a summer's night in Normandy, a new-born
baby is left in a basket outside the home of Albert and Jeanne
Arnaud. The childless couple take the foundling in, name
him Jean, and decide to raise him as their own, though his
parentage remains a mystery.

Though Jean's life is never dull, he grows up knowing little
of what lies beyond his local area. Until the day he sets
off on his bicycle to discover the world, and encounters a
Europe on the threshold of interesting times...

ISBN: 978-1-908313-56-0
e-ISBN: 978-1-908313-59-1

The Foundling's War

Michel Déon

translated from the French by Julian Evans

In the aftermath of French defeat in July 1940, twenty-year-old Jean Arnaud and his ally, the charming conman Palfy, are hiding out at a brothel in Clermont-Ferrand, having narrowly escaped a firing squad. At a military parade, Jean falls for a beautiful stranger, Claude, who will help him forget his adolescent heartbreak but bring far more serious troubles of her own.

Having safely reached occupied Paris, the friends mingle with art smugglers and forgers, social climbers, showbiz starlets, bluffers, swindlers and profiteers, French and German, as Jean learns to make his way in a world of murky allegiances. But beyond the social whirl, the war cannot stay away forever...

ISBN: 978-1-908313-71-3
e-ISBN: 978-1-908313-83-6

The Great and the Good

Michel Déon

translated from the French by Julian Evans

Arthur Morgan is aboard the Queen Mary bound for
the United States, where a scholarship at an Ivy League
university awaits him, along with the promise of a
glittering future.

But the few days spent on the ship will have a defining effect
on the young Frenchman, when he encounters the
love of his life.

ISBN: 978-1-910477-28-1
e-ISBN: 978-1-910477-40-3

Watch interviews between Michel Déon and his translator Julian Evans at gallicbooks.com